RED DUST AND BARBED WIRE

MAX THORNTON

Published in Australia by Silverbird Publishing Pty Ltd.

First published in Australia 2025
This edition published 2025
Copyright © Max Thornton 2025
Cover design, typesetting: WorkingType (www.workingtype.com.au)

The right of Max Thornton to be identified as the
Author of the Work has been asserted in accordance with the
Copyright, Designs and Patents Act 1988.

All rights reserved. No part of this publication may be reproduced, stored in a
retrieval system, or transmitted, in any form or by any means without the prior
written permission of the publisher, nor be otherwise circulated in any form of
binding or cover other than that in which it is published and without a similar
condition being imposed on the subsequent purchaser.

ISBN: 978-1-7644282-0-0 (paperback)

The author acknowledges that many hands have brought his books to life: the editors who polished every sentence, the designers who crafted its cover and the supportive network of friends, family and readers who have championed his writing journey from the very beginning. It takes a village to bring a book into the world, and this book and others are a testament to that collaborative spirit. May they all have all earned a place in heaven.

ALSO BY THIS AUTHOR

This book is dedicated to the little people in my head
who talk to me and tell me what to write,
and to my wife who lives with us.

The gentle breeze was blowing across the fields on either side of the long drive, down through the evergreen peppercorn gums to the large two-storey, mud brick and timber homestead. The tops of the white paper daisies were gently swaying like a thousand small young girls dressed in white bonnets dancing to the tune of an early spring day. Beneath was a lush green carpet of grass thanks to the access of an abundance of fresh water from the Great Artesian Basin. (It contains about 65 million gigalitres of water and underlies a portion of the Northern Territory, including the Simpson Desert, and covers 1.7 million square kilometres of eastern Australia. It is Australia's most significant hydrological system.)

The homestead was a welcoming sight after staring at and driving through three hundred kilometres of red earth gullies, ditches and outback tracks since leaving Tennant Creek five hours ago. The homestead and surrounds were like an oasis in the middle of nowhere, but most parts of the station's approximately three thousand square kilometres of outlying areas were a dry harsh, barren and unforgiving country. Even then, the artesian wells mostly supplied just the cattle's water requirements from one location to another.

A cloud of red dust was thrust into the air behind Riley's vehicle as he drove alongside the station's compacted earth airstrip. As he got closer, the harsh red landscape changed into a softer green. The poddy calves, with no mother cow to feed them, were being fed from buckets by small Aboriginal children who giggled when the calves sucked their hands into their toothless mouths. There were the familiar smells of fresh cattle manure and dry hay coming from large hay barns. The drone of machinery working could be heard close by and not far away, among a cloud of red dust, a herd of Brahman bulls, bellowing their displeasure, were being pushed into a stockyard by a handful of stockmen and Indigenous jackaroos on horseback.

Entry to the large main homestead yard was through an impressive high stone archway. Riley knew it well – he had fallen off the top of it many times as a small boy. He watched as the two border collies and three cattle dogs sniffed and piddled on all the wheels of his four-wheel-drive Land Cruiser.

So, this is the infamous Double Diamond outback cattle station, he said to himself, *with the rumours that no one is ever seen again, once they've visited or worked here.*

He had never heard so much bullshit from those in authority he worked with in the big smoke. It wasn't unusual to hear that a shearer, jackaroo or roustabout travelling through this harsh and unforgiving country on motorbikes or horseback from one station to another was never seen or heard from again, with many explanations how that could occur. But his first impressions were that it looked like any other normal Australian outback working cattle station. But it was early days, and he had not heard all the stories and campfire myths that seemed to have grown and spread throughout the district.

Riley had not been here for quite some time. In fact, Riley had not been here for a very long time. He took a deep breath, and his spirit and the land and the station he had long ago called home became one again. In just a short time, the outback had pushed the city mood and intolerance out of his system and put him back within himself. This mysterious and vast land quickly became part of him again, a land of unspoiled beauty where nature makes the rules, and those that live there abide by them. The outback is like a mother to those who work with and love her, and it's never too late if you love someone or something. Riley hoped his love wouldn't be too late.

In a loud voice, as if there were people listening, he said, 'This is my land and your land. It belongs to all who live and abide by its simple rules. How hard can that be to achieve?'

Double Diamond station had been in the Roper family for more than a century, and they had managed to stay in front of the ever-changing management and breeding procedures, along with the changing rules of the country in the early 1980s when many discussions on land rights and immigration persisted. The 1980s were difficult years with double-digit inflation and high unemployment. However, the station had stayed in front of the curve, having the ability to anticipate and respond to change effectively. Although the station was still owned by the Roper family, Spencer Roper and his wife Aileen had long ago passed, it was now 2025 and the station was being managed and run under contract by a New Zealand company called Wallaroo Consolidated Pastoral Companies. The station staff and employees had changed many times since Riley's days. Only some of the old loyal homestead staff would still be here and familiar with who Riley was. But there were dark secrets still here from the past – the failed love and passion as a small boy he had held for the woman who hardly knew he existed, her sister who almost despised him, the youngest sister of the three sisters who silently loved him and adored the ground he walked on …

A woman wearing a blue checked top and a long white apron approached his car from the homestead. Riley saw her coming and was now embarrassed he had let himself get carried away in the moment, but he did love this place that he had so long ago called home – and so long ago where he had been unknowingly loved. This is where it had all begun, and Riley had suddenly come to terms with the fact that this is where it would all end.

As the woman got closer, she started running, tears running down her face.

'Jesus, is that you, Riley?'

CHAPTER ONE

t was an early, brisk morning at an isolated cattle station in Australia on Sunday, 14 September 1980, the time of year when most things with four legs are born on farms and outback properties. But in a small room in the married stockmen's quarters, something with two legs came into the world. The parents, Nobby and Gwendolyn, certainly weren't living the life of Riley, but they gave him that name anyway. Riley was one of many children born on remote cattle stations, fathered by stockmen and their wives and in some cases with Aboriginal women. In most cases, the children lived their entire lives on the station and grew up to become homestead maids, kitchen staff, cooks, handymen, stockmen, bore runners or mechanics or the younger ones as jillaroos or jackaroos.

When Riley was four, he wandered around under the care of the women who lived in the stockmen's quarters and didn't work in the main homestead. Spencer and Aileen Roper had a two-year-old daughter who had been born on Tuesday, 4 May 1982 amid much fuss in the homestead after the Royal Flying Doctor Service arrived from Tennant Creek. They called her Jessy and, unlike Riley, she had the best care at her disposal. This is not to say that Riley wasn't looked after, but he was simply seen as one of the workers' children whose chances of advancement in the world was minimal compared to those born in the main homestead with connections throughout the cattle breeding society. Occasionally, he was allowed in the main homestead with one of the kitchen ladies where he met and sometimes played with Jessy.

CHAPTER TWO

The station had two Robinson R22 helicopters to find the cattle, commonly known as heli mustering. Depending on how far away the cattle were located, the heli mustering was accompanied by four-wheel-drive vehicles, dogs, motorbikes and stockmen on horseback. The system used was never the same due to weather conditions, cattle distance and difficult locations.

A spotter Robison had been sent up the day before. The cattle were only seventy kilometres out – well, most of them were. The Robbies had pushed them in closer where ground mustering had now taken over. A dark shadow of red dust appeared on the horizon and the pounding of cattle and horses' hooves on the surface of the hummock grassland plains could be heard. As the dust got closer, the shape of the horses and riders could be seen, their faces covered in red dust and weathered by the outback sun, and the large herd of cattle bellowing their displeasure at being pushed along towards the Double Diamond station.

The cattle were predominantly Brahman with some Santa Gertrudis and other drought master breeds, all suited to the hot conditions in the territory. Breeding stock like Angus and Hereford were at their best towards the second grazing season of about twenty-two months of age but would not survive in the harsh outback environment. Livestock and financial lessons were learnt very quickly in the 1980s, and those who were born into the family had access to this sort of knowledge.

The ground crew had been up early, as always, to get the equipment ready. The Robbies had just lifted off again after refuelling to look for strays, Spencer flying one and his second pilot and good friend Gary Bird, whom they all called Feathers, flying the other.

'I'll take the west half for eighty kilometres. I'll leave the east to you, mate,' Spencer said.

'Roger,' said Feathers. 'When we are finished checking for the strays here, I'll go out and check the emergency forty-four-gallon avgas fuel drums if you like.'

'No problem,' came the reply. 'I'll check on the bore runner in the west if you check the one on the east. They have been out now for two weeks and should be starting their return.'

'Roger. Will do.'

Spencer thought a bore runner's job was a lonely occupation. They were alone for long periods of time in the outback with a big responsibility. They needed to be mechanically capable and fit so as to repair and maintain bore pumps and fittings and keep the pumps refuelled. They carried a multitude of spare parts and equipment, food water and radio equipment if they needed something flown out to them.

There was lots to do – checking water levels at wells and pumps, keeping undergrowth and bushes clear of water access points, checking for downed fences, repairing broken boundary barbed wire fences, checking for cattle too far from the main herd and injured and dead cattle with poddy calves that would die if not found.

He admired those who did it. and particularly doing it for the lousy award rate they got – $202 a week – although he always paid them extra, and he gave them the time off from the station that conditions allowed for. He also admired the talent of the mechanics who could keep trucks, tractors and heavy machinery going on wire and home-made welded bits of steel, fuel filters using women's stockings, cracked distributors caps sealed with nail polish, gear change linkages replaced or repaired with fencing wire. He owed them most of his current day-to-day mechanical knowledge.

They were all of them amazing Aussie blokes, and he was bloody proud to know them all. They might not have lived in or had access to the main homestead because of the unfortunate but definite social line drawn in the sand, simply because of wealth or income. Those who came knew what station life was all about and where they would have to fit in. Most of them came from the same social level they had left, so they fitted in very quickly. They had their own community within the station and their own close friends who all ate in the large stockman dining facility separate from the house. It was all like a separate small village.

Christmas Day was the only time that all station staff and the Roper family ate together. The weather was always a typical thirty-seven degrees Celsius and very humid, so the party was held outside when the evening temperatures had come down to a manageable twenty-five degrees. Beef on the spit was always the main meal. This was the time when many of both sexes had free time and when romances were formed.

By Christmas 1988, Riley was eight, Jessy was six and her sister Clara had been born on 10 March that year. During the evening at the party, everywhere Jessy went, Riley followed. He was just ... well, he didn't know what it was, but he was fascinated by her.

'What do you want? Why do you keep following me, Riley?'

'Oh, I don't know. Just to see where you were going and to have someone to talk to.'

'Well, go away and find someone else. You're annoying me. Go on, scoot.'

Spencer and Aileen sat quietly together with a glass of wine each. She whispered in his ear, 'I love you, Spencer, so be very careful. I know how busy and hectic the next few months will be.'

And she was right. The December to February period was the busiest time for cattle mustering and processing, drafting, branding, ear tagging, castration and vaccination. The best bulls were selected to be placed in specific grazing areas. Cows were checked for pregnancy, and in general all stock was separated in age, sex and health, for treatment for the sick or injured animals, or for the oncoming sales in July with the Northern Territory Government Department of Agriculture and Fisheries. All this among the many other maintenance tasks like broken fencing, done in readiness for the oncoming breeding season. Stations could also conduct their own private cattle sales at any time to manage their herd numbers or to make the most of market fluctuations.

CHAPTER THREE

The foreman of the home maintenance and machinery shed equipment was a unmarried employee who had his own stash of whisky hidden away in his hut. Apparently a good worker, but most people at the station held the opinion he was way out here to hide from something. His body language seemed to tell that he was hiding, and he was far too educated and astute to want to be here in the middle of nowhere. His real name was Steven Slowgo, his nickname was Bolta and most station workers only communicated with him when they had to. Even when speaking to Spencer, he was polite but short.

Riley was now ten. After doing the small jobs he had been allocated, like everyone else on the station had been, he was free to wander around and watch and learn. Bolta was driving the tractor lifter with bales of hay up as high as the lifter would allow in the large hay shed and out yard. He had a young Aboriginal jackaroo working with him, climbing on top of the bales to straighten them as they got higher. When the bales had reached their maximum height and the jackaroo was climbing down, his head was crushed by the lifter that was also coming down. Riley was hiding behind some loose bales on the ground. He watched Bolta lift the jackaroo onto the hay bale lifter and drive away. Riley sneakily followed him and watched him tip the boy's body into one of the old sewer wells, which Bolta filled in with a tractor and a bucket attachment the next day.

Suddenly he was grabbed by the neck with a large, strong, hurtful hand.

'If you have seen anything or speak of anything to anyone, I will squash your head with this tractor bucket, young Riley.'

He lay in bed all night worrying about what to do. *Jesus*, he said to himself, *I don't want to die!* so he said nothing. When his mother wasn't present, he had his own version of his prayer, now I lay me down to sleep, a bag of peanuts at my feet. If I should die before I wake, give them to my mate Jake. The Aboriginal boy was listed as having gone walkabout, and it was never spoken about again.

* * *

On Thursday 25 August 1990, Spencer and Aileen had their third daughter. They called her Maxine, and she was the baby of the Roper family, the youngest of the three girls. Riley did the sums in the red dirt with a stick; he would be ten years and eleven days older than Maxine.

Dulcie, the station cook, or kitchen manager, was responsible for preparing the meals and cooking them for station workers, staff and any guests who arrived. Jessy and Clara loved her. Clara was only two and really only hung around the kitchen because her older sister Jessy did, but it was rewarding as she just filled her mouth with what she was given. Though they weren't in the kitchen to watch Dulcie's magic when she was cooking, they were always the first ones there for the taste test. Jessy was the meanest where Riley was concerned. She would take what she was given from the kitchen just to find him and eat it in front of him.

'You're not getting any of this. You're a sook and you've always got a runny nose and pimples. No one even likes you, and I've told all the other kids you poo and wet your pants', which of course wasn't true. Riley couldn't understand how someone he had that puppy love for could be so hurtful and spiteful.

*   *   *

The years rolled by too quickly. Christmas 1995 was upon them. Spencer and Aileen were in their late sixties now and the girls were growing fast. Jessy was thirteen, Clara was ten, and Maxine was five.

Riley was fifteen. He was seen by Spencer as a clever kid who had natural talent. He had been up in the Robbie chopper with Spencer and Feathers on many occasions and could almost fly the thing himself. Spencer and Feathers decided to give him some actual flying training. They gave him books on physics, practical training and theory study, including aerodynamics, navigation, meteorology, flight rules and early operational planning, all of which he excelled in.

He was big and strong for his age and was well liked by all at the station, despite Jessy's catty rumours about him. All of them admired him except the girl he had the hots for, made worse by the fact that her father and Feathers, whom she called Uncle, spent so much time with him. She, for some unknown reason, had no time for him, yet, each time he was near her, his heart leapt out of his chest; the chemical reaction was for him unexplainable. But deep down, he knew he was wasting his time. Maybe that awesome feeling that he felt when she was near was simply common sense leaving his body, and it was time to accept the fact that, for some reason, she simply despised him. So he focused his thoughts now to achieve his dreams of flying, and thought, *Roper or not, if she doesn't change her attitude towards people and life, she is not going to achieve a single thing.*

Then there was Clara and Maxine. Maxine was only five but an adorable kid who followed Riley everywhere he went and would tell him ten times a day, 'I really like you, Riley'. Clara was a beautiful young girl with the bluest of eyes and hair of gold, her lips were a soft pastel red, she had the voice of a songbird and a freckled smile that drove Riley crazy. Why was someone so nice so spiteful, and why did she despise him? He would never understand her. He would learn later in life that a flower in a minefield was still a flower, but you needed to be careful where you walked. She was at at that difficult age of ten where everything she wore mattered. She had special clothes to wear hanging around the kitchen, like handmade aprons. Everything about her had to be perfect to the point where she would take extra time to sort her dress out before she sat at the dinner table, whereas Jessy was often told to go away and come back suitably dressed.

Maxine sat on her pile of cushions at the table and just smiled and took it all in. Maxine thought the dinner table was the best time of the day apart from feeding her beloved Arabian stallion foal Jed, whose breeding name was Jedarie.

She said to herself, *Because I'm the youngest, no one thinks I'm listening or can understand what they're saying.*

But even as young as she was, she was gathering valuable information and she took great delight watching her older sister Jessy's face when her father spoke of how talented Riley was. At five years old, she was, of course, too young to imagine what might become of her infatuation of Riley.

CHAPTER FOUR

The following year, Spencer told Riley's parents that he needed to see them both in his office in the main homestead.

'Nobby,' Gwendolyn said, 'have you done anything that would cause this? We've never been up there before.'

'No, but we're here now and about to find out what he wants.'

'We're probably getting fired.'

'Ah, there you are,' said Spencer. 'Please come in and sit down.'

'I hope we've done nothing wrong,' Gwendolyn said.

'Don't be ridiculous, woman. You both are among our best workers. No, it's your boy, Riley, I wish to talk to you about. He's done nothing wrong either. Please just sit quietly and listen to what I'm going to propose to you. Riley is a talented heli pilot far beyond his age, but he must get his official licence before he can fly here by himself. The station needs a third helicopter for mustering and general work, and I would like its pilot to be Riley. The training we have given him will put him way in front of any others who may be on the course. He needs to go back to Tennant Creek to complete a hundred and five hours of theory and practical training. The cost will be fifteen thousand dollars.'

'Shit!' said Nobby, 'we haven't got that sort of money.'

'I know you haven't,' said Spencer, 'so this is what the station is proposing. We will pay ten thousand dollars for his travel and accommodation in Tennant Creek and in Alice Springs for his final exams. I think the boy needs to know that his parents think enough of him to help with the financial arrangements, don't you?'

'Well, we would be over the moon if we could manage that, but even that is way more than we have.'

'Then this is how we will do it,' said Spencer. 'You will drop to half pay for two months and the boy gets no work money allocated while on the course. His wages will double when he qualifies, and it will be up to you if you need him to pay you back that loss. I'm hoping that won't happen. The boy needs to know his parents realise he is special and deserves to be supported by them. He will pay you back in kind now and who knows what else in the future. No one should go through life without giving another person a helping hand to reach the top of their life's hill.'

Riley knew nothing about any of these arrangements; it was all still in the early planning. He had not been booked on the course yet and his parents had been told to keep it to themselves for the time being.

Listening outside of her father's door was Jessy. She was livid, torn up with anger about what she was hearing was happening to that shithead Riley. What did he have that she didn't? He didn't deserve all this special treatment. His father was just one of the common workers and he was also one of the commoners.

No, she would go away and devise a plan to put an end to all what she heard her father say was "helping someone up the hill". Riley wasn't going up any hill helped by the Ropers if she had anything to do with it.

CHAPTER 5

Jessy questioned herself about her hate for Riley. It was really all about male dominance, wasn't it. He was the one who was shoving it in her face, this pimply-faced kid she had grown up with. She now realised he would have all the opportunities in the outside world while she would be stuck in the feminine niceties of lace and satin, a married wife listening to men like Riley while making sure the special occasion dinners went off perfectly, and then being shoved off while they had their cigars and pompous discussions. No, no, that was never going to be her life! She was one of those who was always going to do what she wanted, not what was necessarily right, and to that end, some stockmen had already had their hands down her pants and top. 'It's my body', she would say, 'and my choice.' Aileen and Spencer had no idea what she was doing when she was outside the bounds of the homestead.

'Come here, young lady.'

She looked up to see Bolta packing a four-wheel drive Land Cruiser and walked over.

'I'm going out to Lizard Channel. Ever been there?' he said.

'No, I've never been anywhere.'

'Well, jump in and I'll show you. I have spoken to your parents.'

'Okay.'

Two hours along the way, he said, 'Oh, and by the way, we won't get there till tomorrow, so we will be gone overnight.'

That was the exact moment she knew she was in big trouble.

When they eventually stopped for the night, it was dark. Bolta made up a bed in the back of the vehicle and tried to get Jessy inside. She managed to break away, calling out, 'You are a pig!' and disappeared into the dark.

* * *

While it was humid and hot all year round at the station, they were now in the wet season when movement by foot or vehicle was difficult. It was their busiest time with the herd. The mustering choppers were an integral part of everyday activities, and now they had three of them. The station had a large radio shack where the children did their schoolwork over the air. It was also used to contact the Flying Doctor for medical issues. There was a 406 MHz radio used for communication with the helicopters and vehicles.

Riley organised call signs, Wallaby 1, 2 and 3. Spencer thought they was unnecessary but humoured him and went along with it. Wallaby 3 was Riley. The decision had been made that day while they had a chopper in the air. They would service the other two Robbies, meaning they still had some aerial coverage.

Riley was following what they called the Lizard Channel, about two hundred and eighty kilometres from the station. 'Shit, he said, 'where's all the fuel gone? I won't get back with only twenty litres,' so he called it in over the Kanard 406 radio pack, transmitted on 406 MHz.

'Double Diamond, Double Diamond, this is Wallaby 3 ...'

He kept calling, with no response. He finally had to descend, landing on some high ground among a small amount of vegetation. He wasn't worried about surviving as all three choppers carried basic emergency gear should they go down: in the three-day ration pack was water, dehydrated food packs, matches, chocolate bars, coffee and teabags, bully beef, a thermal blanket and first aid kits.

Examining the chopper, he discovered a small hole neatly drilled in the aluminium fuel tank that had gone through to the bladder, and the 406 MHz radio antenna had been snapped off. How could someone do this to him? He was only nineteen, not long enough to have enemies who would want him dead.

Then the rain came, belting down in flashing sheets like sharp spears, rebounding off the thermoplastic of the cabin chopper. Then, in a whisper of time, it changed to a gentle pitter-patter to bring nature's magic to dampen the red pathways of this dry land. It had such an effect on Riley that he imagined lying down to die here restfully with the stars to watch over him ...

He jumped out of the Robinson and said out loud, 'Bullshit! While a nice thought, I'm not ready by a long shot for that!' and he set himself up for the long night ahead.

CHAPTER SIX

n the dry season, the Lizard Channel was a dry, red, sandy gully with the top of its banks knocked down by heavy machinery here and there to allow vehicles to cross. But right now, there was a torrent of water coming down the gully, carrying with it dead animals, large logs, everything that happened to be lying in the gully upstream before the wet season's heavy rain. The locals called it a deluge. The Noongar language in the Territory refers to rain as Midjal, and the wet season (lasting from December to March) as Gudjewg.

He woke the next morning to find six small brown eyes and three runny noses pressed up against the plexiglass of the chopper cabin. Gleaming white teeth smiled at him. They were the children of the Waramungu people, the traditional custodians of this area, and the tribe must have arrived while he was sleeping. The elders of the tribe took him downstream to where a woman's body had washed up among branches and other rubbish.

'No! No!' he cried. 'Christ, she was only seventeen. How did she get way out here?'

It was Jessy's body, broken and twisted from being smashed into the banks, logs and branches as she was pushed downstream by the torrent of water. Together they removed her from the water and covered her with the thermal blanket.

There was nothing to do now but wait for the station people to come looking for him.

* * *

Aileen hadn't been well for some time and had spent most of the past year reading a book on the veranda. Spencer knew the time he had left with his beloved wife was limited.

Spencer had been conducting a scheduled radio check to Wallaby 3 with no response. 'Where is that bloody tomboy daughter of ours? No one knows where she is, and she's not been seen since yesterday. Who knows what she is up too? She has been a bugger of a child all her life. But something's not right. Too late to go out now. We will lift off first thing tomorrow morning.'

All the station vehicles had large numbers painted on their roofs so the chopper could call them and give them instructions during musters. Bolta was driving number four, and the pilots knew the numbers off by heart and who would be driving them. Both choppers lifted off and headed out. They called again but still no response.

'I'll go round by Lizard Channel,' said Spencer, 'and you go via the Drovers Hut and swing back through the middle. That way, we'll cross and cover a three-hundred-kilometre area ... Yes, I've got him ... There, he is down there at Lizard Channel ... He looks okay, and the chopper looks okay as well. The whole bloody Warumungu tribe are there as well. I'll land, and you skip over as well.'

When he saw who was under the thermal sheet, his tears were hot and endless for his child that not long had become an adult. They tried to pacify him, with little success. Riley took Spencer's hand, and they both leant against an ancient white gum. Nothing was making sense anymore and all the help in the world was not going to stem the howling pain that was going through Spencer's body. The worst part was still to come – how to tell Aileen. And the biggest question hadn't been answered: how and what was she doing way out there.

They landed back at the station. Dulcie was waiting. Dulcie was seventy-six years old and had been born on the station. She was the oldest and most valued personal staff member. Double Diamond blood ran in her veins.

She said, 'I am so very sorry. While you were all gone, Aileen passed away quietly, reading a book on the veranda today.'

Riley said later the only good about that was she didn't have to know about Jessy. Both choppers had now landed and Riley made himself scarce. He wasn't part of the family, particularly this part. That he had lost a daughter and his long-time wife and companion in the same day was just too much to bear and had put a knife in his heart. He knew he would be sad forever and that Double Diamond would never be the same again.

The funeral notices went out around the district and neighbouring stations, as far away as Alice Springs, as the Ropers were well known and liked. The police air wing would be there tomorrow with detectives to sort out Jessy's unhappy circumstances and a small Jetstream fixed-wing aircraft would be arriving with a forensic team and the coroner. Vehicles would be sent out to the red dirt runway to collect them.

The old wooden sign above their heads as they moved into the burial site said, *Roper's Silent Valley grave site. Please close the gate.* The old broken headstones were leaning towards each other like the families below, great-grandparents and family members, all withered and shrunken like the leaves on the ground above, but the headstones had fulfilled their promise and watched over the deceased. Over a hundred locals, relatives and friends had flown in for the mother's and daughter's funerals, which had been held in the main homestead. There was minimal work done that day to allow the station employees to attend, as there wasn't one person who hadn't adored Aileen. Sadly, most of them would not have known Jessy, or had even seen her.

The small silent cemetery had never seen so many people, who were quietly waiting for the bodies to arrive, all thinking of happier times with the deceased. The two girls, Clara now eleven and Maxine nine, stood with the man they called Uncle Feathers holding their hands. Maxine would have rather been holding Riley's hand, and her nine-year-old mind kept telling her she would marry him one day.

Riley stood under a peppercorn tree, having difficulty understanding what life meant. What he was seeing right now was that the earth was the only thing that would last forever, and even then, he got no answers when he questioned why life could be gone in such a short space of time, and yet at times seem indestructible, without remorse. The tears here today would blind the sun. And just as summer begins with spring, death begins with birth.

He quietly said to himself, *God speed to you, Aileen, to a restful place full of harmony. You were my favourite lady, and an inspiration to the ladies of Double Diamond.*

CHAPTER SEVEN

Station work went on as usual amid a sullen tone, but this, too, would pass, like most unhappy occurrences that seem to wither away with time and life's many changes.

A thousand cattle were being mustered into multiple yards. They were primarily brought in once a year for health checks, counting the herd size, and in some cases selecting which would be sold at market.

Wallaby 3 was tasked with what Spencer called a back-up fly, looking for those that had been missed and left behind. The deliberate damage that had been done to Riley's Robbie had been photographed by the police and had now been repaired. From the air, he could see the many old and new dirt tracks graded over the years due to flooding. If you weren't there when the tracks were done or you constantly moved around in this area, you could get hopelessly lost, unless you were lucky enough to pick a track that actually went somewhere. As he flew, he wondered who the unsavoury bastard was who had drilled his tank and broke the aerial. He knew Jessy hated him, but surely her hate didn't go that far.

Up ahead was a black Land Cruiser marked with a number four on the roof. It was sitting on the south bank of Ironbark Crossing, which had undergone a mesmerising transformation: the parched red sand was giving way to fast moving water. The only sign of life outside the Land Cruiser was a spinifex hopping mouse trying desperately to swim to the other side. Whoever it was in the vehicle, there was only one thing to decide – drive in, die or stay out to live another day.

This vehicle was probably how Jessy got out here. Riley decided not to call it in just yet. He circled and waited.

Each of the station vehicles used to muster or move among the cattle was armed with a rifle to put a sick animal down that was too far away to save or for protection from a big angry male red kangaroo. Nobody went anywhere in the outback stations without some sort of protection. The list of poison biting predators was considerable. The three choppers were no different. They were all armed with long range rifles.

There was no movement from the vehicle, so Riley decided to land and check it out before he called it in. He took his rifle and crept up to the vehicle. His adrenaline went up by a hundred per cent when he saw who it was – Bolta, that bastard who had killed the boy and buried him in the sewer well.

He was fast asleep. Riley bashed him across the head with his rifle.

The vehicle was parked with its front wheels on the edge of the bank's crossing. The torrential rushing water was caving the bank in. Suddenly Land Cruiser number four slid into the water and disappeared downstream, along with the unconscious Bolta. As the vehicle slowly sunk, watched by the Aboriginal tribe and Riley, he called it in. Within the hour, the outback crossing was a beehive of activity with police choppers, police four-wheel-drive vehicles, a woman and a man from the local press who were just dickheads in the way, and who knew how many others who had no right to be there, clogging up the investigation to make a name for themselves and justify their existence with whover it was who paid their wages.

*   *   *

Father Time was determined to wait for no one, and the spring of 1999 was soon upon them, the never-ending cycle of cattle care beginning again.

The veterinarian surgeon had flown out for a week of testing for anthrax and respiratory diseases among the hundred Brahman and few mixtures in the yard closest to the homestead. The room to move around among the cattle in the yard was minimal, with actually no room for a mouse. Some Brahman cattle are naturally polled (without horns) but most generally have horns that curve upwards and backwards, and at this station, dehorning was a common practice, removing the tips to prevent injuries to rest of the herd, and it was quite daunting if you were between them.

Clara and Maxine were sitting on the top rail of the cattle yard. Maxine was telling Clara how much she loved Riley and went to bed dreaming of starlight rendezvous with him. Clara was telling Maxine she was an idiot when she fell off the rail in the yard among the cattle. Amazingly, the cattle seemed to know the danger to the small girl and tried their best not to harm her, but there were just too many of them crammed in the small yard. Some of the cattle panicked, and she was kicked and stood on several times.

Spencer and three stockmen jumped in to get her out. She was unconscious but still alive. They laid her on the ground outside the yard, scared to move her any further on the vet's advice. One of the stockmen had received a serious head wound and Spencer, who should never have been in there but everyone knew why, had been badly bruised. The Flying Doctor was on his way.

Riley said to Dulcie, 'All this is beginning to turn a wonderful station experience for people into a nightmare.'

She was the oldest and most valued personal staff on the station; she was herself 70 years old and had been born on the station, Double Diamond blood ran in her veins.

She replied, 'It's just another brick in this station's latest wall of disaster.'

The Flying Doctor arrived and took Clara, Spencer, and the stockman to Tennant Creek Hospital, a short-stay twenty-bed hospital. After X-rays, scans, and blood tests, Spencer and the stockman were discharged and returned to the station. Clara was transferred to a Jetstream aircraft and taken to Royal Darwin Hospital. Both her legs had been broken, she had a punctured lung and would lose at least one finger on her left hand.

Dulcie was sent to Darwin as her guardian now that Aileen had gone. In Dulcie's absence, the standard of the meals at the station plummeted, reduced to takeaway café style. Maxine had the place to herself now, which meant she could hang around and ogle Riley as often as she wished without her sister's smart-arse remarks.

For the next six weeks, the station returned to its normal stride of long arduous hours of repairing equipment and cattle caring.

CHAPTER EIGHT

Unlike in South Australia where bulls are only joined with females during autumn and spring, due to the expansive size of the land at outback stations, bulls were run with breeding cows all year round, meaning calves could be born anytime. But November, the early beginning of the wet season, was the time most calves were born at Double Diamond. As usually happened, there were poddy calves, whose mother died during birth or refused to accept the calf, to be fed. There were now over three hundred calves wandering with the herd and fifteen poddies brought in to be bottle- or bucket-fed. These sorts of tasks were given to the children who loved it.

Maxine chose a calf for herself to feed and rear to its adulthood. She called it Rybuck, and like her young love for Riley, she absolutely adored it. It was the closest she could get to calling it Riley without people poking fun at her. Roebuck followed her everywhere and ate as many of Dulcie's veggies from the garden as it could while Maxine was picking her own for the homestead. The two of them became inseparable, so much so that Rybuck slept outside Maxine's window at night. The homestead yard gardeners were not impressed, occasionally slipping over in green calf shit. But they understood it was part of the healing process for a small child who had lost her sister and her mother, and Rybuck was an important part of that process.

Clara's legs had healed enough to be out of plaster, but she would be on crutches for some time yet. She was coming home but not before she could take advantage of big-time, big smoke shopping for young ladies' clothes and accessories. Dulcie contacted Spencer who simply said, 'Buy her whatever she wants, and the same goes for you. dear. We will never be able to repay you for your hard work and loyalty over seventy years.'

So, off they went shopping with Clara in a wheelchair borrowed from the hospital for the shopping spree. They couldn't believe the beautiful clothes that were now available, nothing like what you could buy at Tennant Creek. What an opportunity to be wearing something that no one else had ever seen next time they visited Tennant Creek or at the station Christmas party. Clara said she wanted to buy something special for her younger sister, something that would make her more beautiful than she already was and enlarge her fantasies for Riley by dressing up for him – although she thought that Riley had big plans, was someone going places in the world, and she didn't think those plans included her sister. She said to herself, *I think Maxine sees Riley as a bush girl's hope from the crimson dust.* She wanted her sister to be happy and not disappointed if and when that time came, but that was a long way off, and she would make sure Riley didn't break her sister's heart. Riley had no idea that a nine-year-old girl was – well, to put in Clara's words – desperately in love with him. He would just keep pushing on with his long-term goals. He didn't know what they were, but they were a long way from the Double Diamond cattle station.

* * *

'Double Diamond, Double Diamond, this is the Flying Doctor. Foxtrot Delta 02, inbound your location. ETA 15 minutes. On board is a very special patient.'

Clara spoke into the handpiece, 'Hello everyone down there. I'm coming home.'

All those working close to the homestead were now waiting at the airstrip. When the plane came to rest, the first thing off was a snazzy looking wheelchair, followed by Dulcie and the pilot who helped Clara off. The wheelchair had been specially made for the outback terrain with large, rugged wheels for outside and smaller smooth ones for inside that could be changed over in a flash.

The crowd clapped and called out, 'Welcome home! We've all missed you.'

Whether they had or not, these were the sort of words that helped the injured and the healing process, particularly the internal feelings that no one could see. Spencer stood back from the main crowd and admired his daughter's ability to endure the circumstances, and he knew she would be okay. She saw him standing next to Maxine and wheeled herself over.

With tears running down her face, she said, 'Hello, you two.'

Riley had sent an application away to join the police air wing (PolAir) and this plane had the mail he was waiting for. The letter said he would definitely be accepted into the PolAir side of the force; however, he would first need to do his police training at the Academy in Glen Waverley, a suburb of Melbourne. It would be a thirty-one-week live-in course with subjects like law, community, patrol and investigating procedures, report writing, firearms and defensive tactics among others, most of which he would never use as a police pilot. He considered it all a bloody waste of time. He just wanted to fly. *What a load of frog shit!* he said to himself, but he would not let that stop him from flying, so he would do it.

They sent him the necessary paperwork to sign up and he went to Tennant Creek for the medical assessment. All that remained now was to tell everyone he had been accepted, and that was going to be difficult. The Roper family had been so good to him, and without them he would not have had this opportunity. And telling the two girls, well, that would have to be handled separately and diplomatically, to say the least. Riley and Spencer had discussed the issue sometime ago. Spencer had told him to keep it to himself until he was positive about a decision.

Spencer said, 'Not to put you down, Riley, but muster pilots are a dime a dozen. If you decide to go, and I think you should, you will be pursuing an honourable career with advancement opportunities that you won't find here. I don't have a lot of time left of my life. When I'm gone, this place will be run under a licence contract for the Roper family, and I can assure you that you will just be seen as another muster pilot like the rest on the minimum wage the law requires. Don't be a fool, you look after number one, and that, my boy, is Riley. You have been almost like a family to us. Aileen loved you like the son we never had. You are a talented young individual, and I know you're going far.'

Now for the two girls, he said, 'I'm not so old that I don't see what has developed over the years, but I think you have been too dumb or preoccupied with what's been happening. So, before you tell the girls, you need to know that they both love you, Riley, and will be sad to see you go. However, Maxine is very different. Although only nine years old, I suspect her love for you is way past the puppy love for her age, and it's going to be very hard not to break her heart.'

Dulcie and Spencer arranged a morning tea in the sunroom in the homestead for themselves, Riley and the girls. Dulcie had made nice warm scones, jam and cream for the occasion that she knew was going to be tearful and sad. Clara, being the oldest sister, had heard on the grapevine that Riley might be leaving soon, and she knew her little sister would be devastated, so she wheeled her chair next to her for the support that would soon be needed.

Jam and scones in the sunroom was not a normal occurrence at the homestead. Over the years, the only thing that she knew about the sunroom was it was only used for special occasions or announcements.

'I know you're pissing off and leaving us,' said Clara. She was quietly pissed off herself for having to be in a wheelchair, so this was an ideal opportunity to take it out on Riley.

He said, 'I have grown up with you both, and you have been my morning and afternoon sunshine, but there is a natural time for a bird to leave the nest, and the bird must do what it was born to do, and, of course, that's to fly. Through everyone's life, there will be arrivals and leavings, hellos and goodbyes. And to you, my little pigeons, I promise I will come back. You just keep yourselves as beautiful as you are, and if my mind ever dulls of a picture of you both, I will come back for a brain photo. And to you my little chickadee, Maxine, I'm coming back to see how lovely you will have grown up to be.'

* * *

Police training:

'Don't speak unless you're asked something.'

'Spit on your boots.'

'Two creases in your shirt.'

'Pretend you like the instructor, who is actually an arsehole.'

'Make sure you will pass the exam that will have nothing to do with you later on.'

Riley became good friends with a bloke, Barry, who insisted on being called Bazza. He was of the same opinion as Riley. He was going to be with the Water Police. Nobody had ever asked him if he could even bloody swim, but as long as he knew how to do the report while he was drowning, he would pass. He made friends also with a man he would remember all his life; Tobias, Toby for short, was going to be a motorcycle cop. He was the perfect size for a position like that, if there ever was one, and the right temperament to give you a second chance for a minor misdemeanour on the road, just a nice bloke who knew the difference between someone who needed a second chance and one who was a pain in the arse to society and the system. Over time, the three of them – air, sea and land cops – became very good friends.

'Today we are on the parade ground all day,' said the instructor.

'What!' said Riley. 'I'm going to the air wing'

He pointed at Bazza and said, 'He's the Water Police. He can't walk on water, yet we're learning how to march. I suggest you teach him to swim.'

'And I suggest you keep your mouth shut, Cadet Riley, or the only flying you'll be doing is out of here.'

They were eventually given some good information somewhat appropriate to their roles. The three of them decided to put up with the other bullshit parts that were being fed to them for the sake of their real career goals. As for the instructors, the career they were in was a dead end, or maybe they were already at the end of their careers.

Finally, the course ended with the usual parade and hats in the air. Riley made a point of telling the fat senior sergeant he was a pig with no human management skills, that he was very lucky he was in a protected environment, and one day, out of the protection of the academy, he might realise his mouth was responsible for his broken nose.

The New South Wales PolAir was at Bankstown airport. They had five helicopters and two fixed wing aircraft. Riley was posted there as second officer due to his logbook hours, but Riley had a lot to learn about the Bell 412EPI helicopters that were configured for search and rescue missions. The fleet had other aircraft, but the 412 was the key part of their operational procedures. And that's exactly what Riley wanted.

*　*　*

24 August 2001. Tomorrow it would be Maxine's birthday; she would be ten years old. The clock on the wall in the outpatients' department at the Tennant Creek Hospital said 4.25 pm. She was waiting with her father who hadn't been well. He had been told to come in as his test results were there. They had flown there in the station's 150 Cessna fixed wing aircraft.

'Thanks for coming in, Spencer.'

'That's okay, Tom.'

They knew each other very well. Doctor Tom had flown out to the station with the Flying Doctor service on many occasions, and had brought the three girls into the world.

'I'm sorry, Spencer, but the test results weren't what we had hoped for. You have stage four pancreatic cancer. There is no cure. You should go back now and get your personal effects in order. You probably have six months. I'm so sorry, Maxine, there's nothing more we can do for your dad.'

Spencer told the girls that he would have talks with the Wallaroo Consolidated Pastoral Company and the family lawyers about taking over the running and administration of Double Diamond.

'Papers will be drawn up to make Dulcie your official guardian. The family will still own the station, and you girls will live in the homestead as long as you wish. Profits after expenses will go into a shared account for you both. Wallaroo will have two five-year contracts, by which time you will both have turned twenty-one, and any decision what comes after that will be yours.'

Spencer passed away four months later and was buried next to his wife Aileen in the Silent Valley, with just the girls and station hands in attendance. The older you get the fewer friends you have, as most have died along the way.

*   *   *

The girls had continued with the School of the Air to finish their education. Both Maxine and Clara were very bright and, considering where they came from and the restrictions on education that was no fault of theirs, their level of knowledge and perception of what was possible was extraordinary. Clara was now seventeen and had been accepted into the University of Queensland. Maxine, brought up among cattle and animals where life and death were the accepted occurrence though only fifteen, was mentally and physically more like twenty-five. She had not long ago had to say goodbye to Digger, her beloved cattle dog who was born the same day she was. She had decided she would stay at the station and wait for Riley, who had said he would come back to see her. He had written twice but with no return address. She would wait as long as it took; her thoughts were of him every passing day. Her father had told her many times that 'you have to be who you are in this world, not what others want you to be', and that's exactly what she was doing. She loved him desperately, and one day he would love her too. She knew that in her heart so, yes, she would wait.

CHAPTER NINE

Benjamin Andrew Forester thought the time his parents had spent choosing his name had been a bloody waste of time when even people he hardly knew, including the second-hand car salesman, called him Ben. He was the same age as Riley, twenty-five, and was studying at Queensland University to one day become a paediatrician. He was in his third year, studying integrated medicine, surgery and pathophysiology.

He had just met Clara in one of the food outlets on campus and they were having a sandwich together. She was living on campus in one of the dorms; he was staying with his mother who lived close to the university. His father was in the police force somewhere in New South Wales. Clara had excelled in her year 12 and she was in her first year of medicine, currently studying anatomy, psychology, biochemistry, pharmacology and microbiology. She was a long way behind him, but she knew he would be a handy friend to help and get advice from along the way. Many people thought they were a pigeon pair as Clara wanted to study women's health and childbirth complications.

At first glance, Ben was your everyday sort of bloke, but his softly spoken words and his passion to heal sick and underprivileged children was amazing. With his devotion and demeanour, he would be like a father and a comfort to the children who were sick, and they would just love him. Well, that's what Clara thought, and she knew she was right.

Meanwhile, at Double Diamond, Dulcie, who had been like a second mum to the kids, had sadly passed away, so Maxine had decided to deal with the day-to-day running of the station. The contract management had a condescending attitude towards her, firstly, because she was a woman and secondly she was young, and the manager's opinion was she should have no say at all. But they were fucked, weren't they. She was one of the two owners who had decided to stay on. She decided to do the necessary subjects at the Queensland University where her sister was and qualify as the Double Diamond and area veterinary surgeon, where her say as the owner and the vet could not be ignored.

Maxine rang her sister and told her she was coming and what her intentions were. She then spoke to the homestead staff.

'While I'm away at university, the contract staff are not permitted in the homestead. None of the day-to-day activities is to be changed, and if they are, you will contact me immediately on this number.'

'Yes, ma'am!' they said.

She had already had run-ins with the contract company station manager, who taken no notice of her requests. Before she left, she told the company through the family solicitors if they didn't get rid of him, the family station owners would be looking for new managers at the end of the contract. He was gone and replaced before she left.

When she arrived at Brisbane airport, Clara and Ben were there to meet her. They hugged, kissed and cried, while Ben stood away from them and gave them their happy time together.

'Well, who's this, then?' Maxine asked.

'He is a very good friend of mine. This is Benjamin. He is in his third year of medicine at the university with me.'

'Do I see things happening here?'

'No, you don't see anything!' said Clara.

'Hello, Ben,' she said, 'nice to meet you. I will be here through the week and fly back at the weekends to look after the homestead and my own responsibilities there.'

Ben said, 'Clara has told me all about you. You certainly don't look fifteen. You are certainly giving yourself a good start in life. Maybe one day I'll come and see Double Diamond with the both of you.'

'I'll look forward to it,' said Maxine.

* * *

The new station manager's name was Mat Hilda; his nickname was Matilda. He was a lot younger than the previous self-righteous bastard who had been given the boot. Mat was a bit of a spunk but nothing compared to Maxine's Riley. He had obviously been told to be respectful and prepared to at least discuss things with Maxine if she wanted.

'She doesn't normally interfere, but she is no dill when it comes to running the Double Diamond cattle station. If you treat her like a young female idiot, you won't last five minutes,' said his second-in-command, a bloke called Darcy.

Well, that was his name at this station. He had worked at stations in Western Australia, all under different names. He was wanted by the police in that state and Tasmania for a hit-and-run accident and was a suspect in a murder trial, but his credentials, on paper anyway, were spotless. He had a devious and sly look about him, but you know the age-old saying, "looks are deceiving" and "don't judge a book by its cover", so there he was in the outback hiding from the authorities.

40

CHAPTER TEN

Riley was enjoying his posting to the Bankstown airport's PolAir, and it hadn't taken him long to get on top of the Bell 412. He would be the copilot for another year and then the seating arrangements up front would change. The callout codes were not unanimous with the other states, and Riley said he wasn't surprised with that, as he thought New South Wales had a competitive brain that insisted on being better than other states, even if it compromised safety. (Nothing between states in Australia is uniform, not even the road laws, or the age of attainment to get a vehicle licence. It's like trying to get two common enemies like the fox and the sheep to play together nicely.)

The call came from police headquarters in Sydney – a small female child and her dog missing at Barrington Tops National Park in NSW, situated in the Hunter Valley between the towns of Scone, Singleton and Dungog. The young girl's name was Megan, she was eight years old and her dog Molly was a black Labrador who went faithfully with her wherever she went.

As they looked at the map, Riley said, 'Look at the size of the search area!'

The park is part of the Mount Royal Range, a spur of the Great Dividing Range. Barrington Tops covers an area of more than 75,000 hectares and is part of the Gondwana rainforest which is more than 83,000 hectares of unspoiled wilderness.

His commander said Molly had gone for a short walk with the dog from where they were camped in the highest campground in the state, surrounded by snow gums. These campsites and places like Gummi Falls, Junction Pools and Wombat Creek were only accessible by four-wheel-drives or on foot.

Megan had been playing with Molly with a stick, and then she was gone. Her parents were beside themselves. They had searched and called but got no response. Megan's father was a well prepared four-wheel driver and camper, so the vehicle was equipped with a satellite phone, and he raised the alarm that same afternoon. This would be Megan and Molly's first night by themselves, if they were still alive. At that time of the year, the nighttime temperature varied from seven to minus two.

The commander said, 'Look at the maps in front of you at the grid references you have been given. You will see they would have gone in along the Link Trail that runs between the Chichester and the Kerripit rivers. Our main rescue site is being set up by the State Emergency Service in a large clearing at Rocky Crossing; you have also been given that grid reference. We will be sending two Bell 412s, and we will be supported by police on motorbikes and horses, along with foot patrols and some locals who know the area. The police bikes will concentrate on the areas around Junction Pools on the Barrington River, so I've been told. There will be an Orders Group at 5.30 tomorrow morning at Rocky Crossing. Pack your bags. We leave in an hour.'

There were over one hundred people at the O Group. The search and rescue commander thanked everyone for their quick response and outlined the order of march.

'Each voluntary team of bushwalkers and locals will have with them a park ranger, a police officer and an ambulance officer; they will work the western side of Junction Pools. The police motorcycle unit will cover the east side as far as Black Swamp. The police on horseback will take the trails and tracks on the south side along and around the Corker Track. PolAir will take all of the north side as far as Forrest Road. Any questions?' There were none. 'Then, good luck. Go and find the little girl and her dog, who have now been out there all night.'

*   *   *

When Maxine returned home after her first semester of fifteen weeks, she was introduced to Darcy, who was the only new "kid on the block" since she had left. She knew outback men, strong and rough, were not known for their handsome appearances, but there was definitely something that said to be very afraid of this man. His mouth exposed brown rotten teeth, all sharp on forward angles, that threatened to bite off his lips. The wind blew his unkempt hair away from a face a mother wouldn't own. His chin jutted out over his largely protruding Adam's apple as if to save it from the sun. He appeared unmistakably sly and mean.

She made a point to talk to Matilda in private and confidently about him. She knew she would need to be very wary of this Darcy.

CHAPTER ELEVEN

Megan kept calling out, 'Molly, you're a naughty girl.' She had walked off the track into the bush where she could hear the dog barking in the distance. Now she had no idea which way went back to the camp, but she kept moving downwards into a gully where she thought she could hear water.

The undergrowth was thick and tore at her legs and arms as she waded through it. The tears were starting to run down her face as she realised she was now hopelessly lost. The sun had disappeared behind the trees and darkness was quickly claiming the day. She remembered her father telling her about the wild pigs in the bush that could rip one to pieces with their sharp tusks. As it got darker, the sounds of the bush, the birds and critters, were gone, nothing except the occasional slither of something underfoot. She stumbled into a small creek of fresh running water, almost concealed by the undergrowth and a fallen tree. At the base of the tree was a large hole and the overhang of the large roots almost covering the hole provided a small amount of overhead cover. She was scared to pieces but, like magic before her eyes, there was Molly licking her face and wagging her tail.

'Now we are both lost.'

Molly snuggled up against her. She was warm and gave Megan a sense of security against any night predators that might come along, and she was soon fast asleep.

When she woke, she could hear helicopters somewhere overhead, and she knew they would be looking for her, but they were nowhere near where she was, and down in the gully, they would never find her.

'Come on, Molly,' she said. 'We have to go back up and find a track to sit on and wait for someone to come along.'

* * *

Riley said to his copilot, 'I think this little girl will be out here another night unless the ground crew find her. Look how quickly the mist is rolling down and softly covering everything in that valley. In an hour, we won't be able to see anything under its blanket. We'll spin back and try and cover those tracks closer to where she left their campsite, but this time we'll pay more attention to the smaller animal tracks ... What's that? Did you see that, or did I imagine it? Let's swing back for another look ... Yes, there it is, a black dog coming out of the scrub onto the track. I don't think the girl will be far away from the dog. This is Sky Eye Charlie Six. Dog sighted at grid 346–178 on small trail leading to Wombat Creek. Over.'

'Sky Eye, this is trail bike 4. Is that you, Riley? This is Toby. Back to you.'

'Well, I'll be buggered!' said Riley. 'Where are you, Toby?'

'A couple of clicks from you. I don't need a grid. Just hover overhead and I'll be there.'

Everyone was on the same frequency so he wouldn't be the only one heading there.

Molly had been bouncing along, sniffing the ground and disappearing in and out of the bush in the sides of the small trail Megan was following. It meandered slightly downhill, and her young brain kept telling her that was better than going up, although she didn't know why at the time. Molly had been smelling animal scents and kept disappearing but would come back out further down the trail, as if she knew exactly where Megan was. And, of course, she did know; she had known Megan's scent from birth. But, further along the trail, Molly had not come out of the bush yet, so Megan left the trail to find her. Molly's leg was caught in a rabbit trap and she was lying on the ground, whimpering. Megan tried time and time again to release her, but the jaws of the trap were too strong for her small hands to open.

Toby arrived under the chopper.

'Sky Eye Charlie Six, nothing showing this location. Over.'

'Stay there, mate, for the four-wheel drives to arrive. She and her dog must be close by.'

When the ground searches arrived, it was close to dark. They spread out in a large circle around the grid reference given by Riley and worked their way inwards.

Megan was trying to comfort Molly when she heard her name being called out.

'Over here, over here!' she called back.

The first one to see her and her dog was a woman who could have been mistaken for her mother the way she hugged and kissed Megan. Molly was released from the trap, and they were both taken for medical check-ups, Molly's first ever ride in an ambulance.

'Sky Eye Charlie Six, this is bike 4. Switch frequency to private.'

Once the switch was made, Riley said, 'Meet me at Young and Jacksons pub Saturday, 6 pm. I'll ring Bazza, if he hasn't drowned yet. Over.'

'Roger!' came the response.

Young and Jacksons, Melbourne's most iconic pub located opposite the landmark steps of Flinders Street Station, was established in 1864 and is a Melbourne icon and mascot for HMAS *Melbourne* and home to the infamous "Chloe". She is the famous nude portrait that has graced the walls of the pub since 1909. Riley remembered his father recalling it as a meeting place, a local watering hole and a place for celebration, a place for romance and a place for good people to share good food and wine. He couldn't wait to get there with his two friends. He had never seen the portrait of Chloe or his police friends for some time, and he was looking forward to it all.

But Riley failed to see what all the fuss and hubbub was all about when he saw Chloe. Maybe there was a big hole behind it and back in 1909, someone had found the painting in the storeroom and hung it up to hide the hole. After a few beers, he was tempted to have a look behind it. Toby and Bazza talked him out of it.

'Buggered if I know. It's just another nude painting, if you ask me, nothing to write home about.'

Bazza said, 'Well, mate, there's a few million people, mostly blokes, that wouldn't agree with you.

CHAPTER TWELVE

Clara and Ben were becoming closer as time went on. He had muscles under his shirt, but not the kind you get from weightlifting, and he always had that grin that boys have when they had done something they shouldn't have. He had stolen Clara's heart without even knowing it. Was this the love she had been waiting for, a love that would cherish and blossom with a timeless passion? How could he not feel the vibes of love that were radiating from her?

She was beginning to understand Maxine's relentless love for Riley who was too dumb to feel the hundreds of arrows that had been fired into his heart over the years by a girl who was far too young for it to be anything than a one-sided affair. Clara hoped hers would not be. She had now turned twenty, and she told herself there was lots of time in her life left, so for now she would concentrate on her studies. Clara was about to start her third year of medicine, and Ben would be finished this year.

Maxine had completed her first year of Doctor of Veterinary Medicine and was on a six-week break before commencing her next year. She had made several friends on the same course who had asked her about the outback and why she preferred there to the city. Maxine said she couldn't deal with the close confinement of living; there didn't seem to be enough personal space for each person.

'I'll always be an outback girl. Australia is a wild place, and the outback is untameable. It's remote and vast and sparsely populated; in other words, bugger all people live there. It's a place of red dust and barbed wire, lush blue desert skies and wide open spaces, and the stars at night lighting up the heavens will send you into your own private dreamland.'

There are occurrences that happen on cattle stations like Double Diamond that are unexplainable and are simply accepted as the norm. The outback is a place where justice is simple and mercy is scarce, and station life just rolls on. She was back at Double Diamond in time for her eighteenth birthday, 25 August 2009. All the original staff had passed away or grown up and moved on, so there was no celebration.

The homestead and its surrounding area were fenced off and some distance from the contractors' housing and kitchen. Some of the workers had their families with them, but Maxine had not had anything to do with them. It was rumoured that the contractors called the homestead area "the kingdom". Some of the original Aboriginal children who had been born and grown up there were still working there as homestead gardeners, cooks and cleaners or were now stockmen or general hands.

Feathers had retired and gone back to Alice Springs. He was now the on-call, or relief, chopper pilot for the tourist flights off the Ghan train during its stopover at the Alice. The contract company at Double Diamond had their own heli muster pilots, whom Maxine had been introduced to. She had also been personally introduced to the upper echelon of the company running the station and often stopped and spoke to the station hands and or their wives. Although she had nothing to do with the running of the station, everyone knew who she was, and they liked her, and Matilda had on special occasions, like someone's birthday, invited her to the workers' parties, which most times she would attend. Matilda was easy to get along with, which meant most times, issues at the station could be sorted out between him and Maxine without involving solicitors and painful legal bullshit occurring.

Bunya, born on the station around the same time as Maxine, had made herself Maxine's personal maid. The bunya, or bunya bunya, is a native tree with edible nuts often found in the outback, and the name had a sense of place with the land, as is always the case when Aboriginal parents name their children. Maxine was glad to be back where she knew she belonged, and Bunya could not stop fussing over her. 'Very happy to have you home, missy.'

The second place she visited was the stables to see her beloved Jed, a magnificent Arabian stallion. When the horse saw her, his large eyes stared and he reared up, grunting and snorting in recognition. Maxine opened the stall door and went in. She began to cry at what she saw. The horse's rump was covered with dry and fresh cuts from whippings. Jed knew who she was and nuzzled its head into her arms. She said to herself, *Whoever has done this is dead. I will kill them.* The Aboriginal stable boy said it was that awful man, Darcy.

She found Matilda. 'Come with me,' she said. 'Look at my horse! Find Darcy. I'm going to kill the bastard.'

'Jesus!' Matilda said when he saw the horse. 'Who could do such a thing?'

A voice behind them said, 'Me, that's who. It's a bastard of a horse that needs to be taught a lesson and how to behave.'

Matilda knocked him down.

'Pack your bags and get out before I call the police.'

'I'm going,' he said, 'but I'll be back to deal with you and the bitch.'

They watched him ride out on his motorcycle towards Tennant Creek.

'Good riddance!'

CHAPTER THIRTEEN

Riley was now a senior pilot with PolAir, having finished his training and gained his fixed wing pilots licence to fly both rotary wing and fixed wing. He had just received his orders to be transferred to Queensland. PolAir had a variety of aircraft in their fleet, some of which Riley would need further training in. These types of aircraft would be spread around Queensland to support the police, depending on location and distance needed to travel to support an emergency. Their aircraft included a Beechcraft 1900D and Beechcraft B300 Super King Air, the 180E, 402B, 421C and S550 Citation Cessnas and a Hawker 850XP jet. The rotary wing aircraft were a Bell 206 LongRanger and the Bell 412 that Riley had so many hours flying in he felt like he was born with it in his cot.

Double Diamond had in the past had an earlier model fixed wing Cessna which Riley had had nothing to do with, and he wondered if they still had it. He also wondered about many things from the past, memories that would remain forever. Where were the girls, Clara and Maxine? Were they still at the station? Little did anyone know he knew Maxine had adored him, but back then she was only a child; compared to her he was an adult. He had places to go and dreams to fulfil when she was still at the stage of running noses, plaits and poddy calves.

He had arrived in Brisbane in time for the Christmas celebrations and had been invited by Bazza (who was working and living in Brisbane) along with other friends and relatives and police from PolAir to the Water Police Christmas party. As usual, he went by himself.

'Ah, there you are,' said Bazza. 'Come with me. There is someone I want you to meet.'

There was a fit looking young bloke standing there with a woman who had her back turned to him talking to someone.

Bazza said, 'Riley, this is my son Benjamin and this is his friend, Cl––'

As soon as the woman heard the name "Riley", she spun around.

'Well, I'll be a lizard's legs!' Riley said.

Clara's thoughts of the past about Riley had somewhat softened and her nasty schoolgirl jealous attitude had long ago gone, so they hugged each other affectionately. The four of them sat down with a drink. There was a lot to talk about. She told him that Maxine had been doing veterinary medicine, but was back at the station doing her second year by correspondence at the University of Adelaide at the Roseworthy campus. She travelled back and forth when required.

'You've just missed her.'

CHAPTER FOURTEEN

A police radio transmission had been received over the station's net that a rough gang of Aboriginal young men were on the loose, terrorising stations and small landowners throughout the area, and a farmer had been shot and had since died.

The gang of Aboriginal youths who found Land Cruiser number four upside down, stuck on a sand bar in what was now a dry creek bed, had no idea that there should have been a body in there. They pushed it back onto its wheels and camped in there for the night, unaware that they were being watched by someone behind a salt bush. Over the past couple of years, there had been reported sightings by different Aboriginal tribes of the Bunyip Man, a boogie man who catches you and drags you into the water. The Bunyip Man was said to be covered in hair, his eyes visible deep within the hair, with large, long fingernails to claw at his victims. He could disguise himself as a tree or a bush and grab you as you walked past. Some of the tribes called this thing the monster of the outback, although only a few had claimed to have seen it. There were many stories told by Aboriginal elders about this Bunyip, but whatever it was, they were scared of it, and children were never left by themselves.

Matilda spoke to Maxine and they both decided, for the women and children's benefit, that for the next two weeks, they would send overnight armed vehicles with radios able to communication back to the station out in a five-hundred-metre circle around the main homestead, station yards and workers' quarters. A code word was given to each vehicle and everyone who belonged at the station, including the children; anyone in the dark not answering to the call 'Double' with the response 'Diamond' was to be shot – no bloody excuses! Any police support was out of the question. They simply made their own discipline outcomes which had little mercy. Four four-wheel-drive vehicles, two workers in each, were deployed each day at sunset, and the men replaced each two hours. It was hard to imagine how anyone could get close to a barren outback station without being seen, but with the artesian water supply close to the homestead, there was an abundance of bushes and tussock weed for predators to hide behind. If they got into the inner circle of the station, who knows what would happen, although they would be outnumbered if they came in that close.

The first week of the outrider security vehicles saw or heard nothing and was a drag on the station's workload. A meeting of all station personnel, including children, was held in the cattle yard. They were told that trip wires were being placed around the inner station area with explosives attached. This area would be known as the red zone and marked by red boundary paint, and the green zone marked with green paint. Nobody was to go further than the green zone line.

The trip wires were now in place, and it was hoped the spinifex hopping mice and small critters would not be large or strong enough to set them off.

Maxine said, 'So, now it's a waiting game.'

*   *   *

The gang sliced up a large goanna for breakfast and headed off in the direction of Double Diamond. There were fifteen of them, so they thought they would have the upper hand, with not enough brains to know these sorts of stations have on average fifty or sixty people to run them. Travelling along some distance behind them was the Bunyip Man.

They could see the outside security lights of the station in the distance ahead of them. They had spread out around the station and on the signal, they would all go in at the same time. With the stealth of a hungry leopard, the cunning of a fox and the brains of a beanbag, they tripped the wire. Eleven of the fifteen were blown to pieces and two of them had their legs blown off.

The whole station was now awake, the men searching for the remaining two gang members inside the inner perimeter. One had set fire to the barn and hayshed next to the stables where Jed and the other horses were going crazy with fear.

Someone called out, 'The sheds are on fire.'

'The horses! Get the bloody horses!'

Maxine ran into the stables. The horses were kicking the stall doors to get out and the two gang youths inside were coming towards her with a machete. A worker, who had climbed up on the mezzanine floor with the hay, threw down a large pitchfork to her. One of the kids kept coming, so she rammed the fork through his neck, pinning his body to the wooden stable wall and killing him. Maxine let the horses out of their stalls, and they bashed and kicked his body as they stampeded past. Nobody noticed the Bunyip Man sneak into the supply room and steal a large bag of food, then disappear. The last Aboriginal boy was never found.

The police investigation team arrived by air, along with the coroner and forensic rubber glove mob. There wasn't much they could do except take statements and remove what was left of the bodies.

57

CHAPTER FIFTEEN

Riley was now thirty-one years old, and Maxine would be turning twenty-one this year. He would send a birthday card to the station and hoped it would find her. He had seen Clara and Ben on several occasions at the different police functions that Bazza invited him to. Ben had been a qualified doctor for some time now, and Clara had one year to go.

Ben and Clare had finally realised they had both fallen in love, and to keep ignoring it was senseless. They decided to do a three-day cruise on the SS *Dream Chaser* to celebrate, then they were going to announce their engagement to family and friends after the cruise. The SS *Dream Chaser* was a retired steamship that had been saved from the scrap metal yard some years ago, and a considerable amount of money had been spent on refitting her as a three-day cruise ship around the local islands. She had a capacity of two hundred passengers and crew. She had travelled many oceans and carried many voyagers over her years, and the way she moved herself through the water now was her unspoken word of thanks for the second chance to do what she was born to do.

Clara and Ben boarded the vessel at Airlie Beach in North Queensland with a couple of hundred other excited passengers and found their bags at their cabin door . The ship was old, but her refit was magnificent, bringing back all the charm of days gone by. The internal carved woodwork stairs and handrails were a credit to the person who had done the intricate work.

The first night out was choppy, but in the morning, Clara said the gentle rocking had put her to sleep immediately. The second night out was typical North Queensland weather, calm and balmy. Most people were still at their dinner tables when the explosion occurred.

A voice came over the speaker. 'This is the captain speaking. The explosion you heard was the boilers bursting. We have significant damage to the hull. Please do not panic. Put your life jackets on and move slowly and quietly to the lifeboats. We are preparing to evacuate the ship.'

An ear-piercing alarm siren sounded. Passengers scrambled back to their rooms for their life jackets. The next explosion came from the engine room and opened up the seams in the stern of the ship's hull, and because she was still moving, the water was coming in through the seams. The old ship would eventually go down by the stern, the captain's estimating in three to four hours.

The radio room sent out mayday calls throughout the maritime net and received immediate responses of help on the way. They weren't thousands of miles off land, which was about a hundred nautical miles away, so response times and the distance were on their side.

Riley was on the afternoon shift at PolAir in Brisbane with five other pilots when the newsflash came about a ship in distress off Airlie Beach. At the same time, the red muster phone rang. Riley was the senior officer that night. He scrambled his and one other long Ranger Bell 412 helicopters and kept the other two pilots available for the fixed wing Hawk if requested. The Bell 412 that the police had were all configured slightly differently to accommodate for emergency equipment and could carry seven passengers and the two pilots.

Unbeknown to Riley, Bazza was on holidays with his wife and grandkids at Airlie Beach. The Water Police there had bugger all for this sort of operation. They had a vessel called the *Damian Leading* which was merely equipped for minor search and rescue, speeding and drink driving, and after hours to find the crew they needed in time … well, good luck with that! Bazza knew his son and Clara were going on one of these cruises, even though they had kept it a secret. Bazza suspected that they were going to soon announce their engagement, so he hadn't want to pry. As he was, like Riley, now in the higher echelons of the force, he got himself involved in the rescue.

It was about an hour and a half to two hours of chopper flying time to the rescue area from Brisbane, which gave the chopper crews ample time to get their winching equipment ready to go. Both choppers had what is called a stokes litter, a specially designed basket metal and plastic woven stretcher, to winch injured patients up to the chopper from difficult locations, along with other standard rescue equipment.

As they got closer, Riley started calling, '*Damian Leading* one, this is PolAir Six Foxtrot One. Over. Pilot Officer Riley. Over.'

'Jesus, Riley, is that you? This is Bazza.'

'What are you doing here?'

'I'm on bloody holidays! We are only a twelve-metre patrol boat, but we will assist where we can. I'm not sure, but Ben and Clara could possibly be on that ship. They were talking about going but I don't know when.'

'Well, if they are, we will get them off along with everyone else'

'Normally this place would be a beehive of pleasure boats and catamarans,' Bazza said, 'but they will all be anchored for the night in one of the coves. And the island passenger transport vessels have done their last run and will be shut down for the night, but they are always on an availability standby twenty-four hours a day for emergencies, so they will be scrambling now to fire up and get to the stricken ship.'

'Steam ship *Dream Chaser*, this is PolAir Six Foxtrot One. Over.'

The answer came back. 'This is *Dream Chaser*. No time for bullshit call signs. There are two hundred passengers on board, and we are going down by the stern. We are listing badly now to port side, can only get the life rafts off on the starboard side.'

Riley said, 'Clear the best space and light it up. The turnaround time for us at a hundred kilometres will be an hour. That's far too long, so this is the plan. The two island ferries are to stand off two hundred metres, and people in rafts off the ship are to go to those ferries. The police patrol boat will get in close and feed the ferries with as many people as they can. We will take seven at a time. I will feed one ferry, and the other chopper will feed the second ferry; that will be fourteen at each pick-up. That way we won't be in each other's way in the dark. ETA is fifteen minutes, so stand by.'

Riley's instructions had been heard by all over the emergency network and all involved acknowledged the instructions.

On board the steamship, children were crying and calling out for their parents, screams of panic had flooded the deck and everywhere were passengers stricken with fear. Some were leaping into the water and others were trying to get the life rafts off the listing port side. The pulleys that lowered the rafts couldn't all release at the same time so six people were hanging down vertically on one cable.

'Jesus!' Riley said, when he saw all the panic.

The helicopters went in one after the other, hovering two metres off the unstable, slowly sinking deck. When the copilot left the chopper to help lift people climbing up to the aircraft, they could take eight people.

Looking at the people waiting on the deck, which was now at a really bad angle, Riley said they would need to do probably another four trips each. The turnaround time should have been fifteen minutes, but some of the older passengers took longer to get them on and off at the other end, so sometimes it was more like twenty-five. When they went back for the last sixteen passengers, they were standing on the deck in water up to their knees. There, looking pale and frightened but bravely waving, were Clara and Ben.

'They're all in,' called the copilot, as he climbed in. They lifted off as the Steamship *Dream Chaser* went down.

CHAPTER SIXTEEN

Over the radio was a police warning that three girls were missing from the surrounding station, a young girl from a farmhouse and two Aboriginal young girls from a nearby tribe. Maxine wondered if the girls had run away together. Were they the ones stealing the food or was it the one Aboriginal gang youth who hadn't been found, because small amounts of food were missing from the shelves of the main station supply room, which had only started happening since the Aboriginal gang attack. It was such a small amount that it didn't seem to worry anyone, and it was food that would keep, like cans of baked beans, bully beef and soup, and small amounts of rice. Matilda had put a padlock on the overhead fuel tanks, as someone had been taking small amounts of fuel as well, hardly noticeable but only discovered because they kept meticulous records of the fuel used. And it only happened every month or so.

* * *

In a cave made from the overhanging sides of a dry creek bed that had been dug in some twenty metres were two Aboriginal and one white girl bound and gagged, but with a small hole just big enough to eat the food that was hanging from a string just within reach of their mouths. There was a water in a container on a string they could swing, using their heads to go past each of them to suck up some water. Outside in the creek bed was a motorcycle, and further up the creek bed were the remains of the owner of the motorcycle, the man known as Darcy. Inside the cave, the Aboriginal girls were blabbering about a Bunyip, who the tribal elders had told them about since they were babies, who at that moment was filling the motorcycle from a can of fuel stolen from the cattle station.

* * *

Most of the machinery and the old ways of doing things had changed, and they had to if the station was to keep up with technology and marketing in 2017 when the use of drones and computerised equipment and farm machinery were being used.

The member for agriculture in parliament had just arrived on a visit to Double Diamond.

'It must be getting close to voting time,' said Maxine, who at twenty-six was now a woman of the world and a qualified veterinarian for the district.

He said, 'So, tell me, Miss Roper, about this station called Double Diamond and why it is a place of importance to Australia's food survival. What can I tell the voters I am supporting in the coming election?'

'Let's get one thing straight. Firstly, it's all first-name basis out here. Keep that perfectly correct crap where you came from. What you would know about agriculture in the outback would be the same amount of smoke I could catch in my bare hand from that burn-off fire over there.'

She asked his pencil-pushing aide, 'What's your name?'

'Thomas.'

'Well, Thomas, do you have a recording device?'

'Yes.'

'Turn the bloody thing on. This land you're standing on is vast and terribly unforgiving, but it's beautiful in its own significant way. The men and women who work these isolated stations are exceptional people. Our arid outback takes up roughly seventy per cent of Australia's land mass but is home to three per cent of the population. It is an integral part of Australia, and who we are and our pastoral capabilities. You are standing where livestock are free to roam and, in some cases, can be born and reach maturity without seeing a human. Water runs to bores, troughs and dams and it can take days or weeks to check them. Mustering is done with planes, helicopter, horses and ground vehicles. This is the land where Burke and Will perished, due to their lack of knowledge of the Australian bush and how to survive in it. This is the land where nature makes the rules, and we keep up if we can. If you spent some time out here during musters and get to really know the stations and the people who work them, you might just get the votes you're after.'

The minister said, 'Well, thanks for those candid comments. We won't be keeping you away from your work any longer. By the way ... who are you?'

She looked him squarely in the eye and said, 'I am the bloody owner.'

*   *   *

The Bunyip Man was now riding towards Double Diamond Station with a ten-litre can strapped to each side of the bike. The twenty-litre fuel tank gave the motorcycle the capacity to travel the hundred and fifty kilometres back to the station to resupply his fuel by stealing whatever he could find. He was super careful when arriving on the outskirts of the station. He had been here and seen what could happen when the station set their security system up. There was no charging in, gung-ho style. He had already seen how that worked out.

He arrived at the station at 2 am, turned off the motorcycle and pushed it in the last kilometre. His first stop was the station ration building. The lock caused him little problems with the iron bar he had to burst it. He was only sorry he couldn't take the supplies he would like; due to his current situation, he took long-life food supplies and small essentials to him like matches and a variety of medical supplies. He had also managed, over the last two visits to the station, to dig in bit by bit under the machinery shed where the explosives were. Once he stole the explosives and his resupply of fuel, there was one other place he badly needed to go – the highfalutin' homestead where she lived.

He had a misconception of the meaning of highfalutin'. The Double Diamond homestead was mud brick and timber. Most of the windows were simply wooden shutters on a stick to hold them open and mosquito netting at certain times or the year was hung up at night. There was nothing to describe the homestead as a manor, and like most of the Australian outback homesteads, while comfortable, it was nothing to write home about. You could be forgiven for thinking how basic and primitive it was on entry, as the furniture was basic and it had a simple concrete floor with no floor coverings due to the red dirt and dust being tramped in on a daily basis. Its only power came from a large diesel generator; there was no such thing as air-conditioning. Long trucks called road trains delivered fuel, machinery and other necessary supplies as required. However, after spending some time in the homestead, you suddenly realised how well, for this hot and unfriendly environment, the house had been designed and in fact was more like a home than a house. Somehow the Double Diamond homestead crept into your soul, and said, *I know who you are and you are welcome to my home and my history.*

The Bunyip Man crept up towards the homestead. He wasn't sure how he would kill her, but there was no doubt he would. He crept around, looking in windows to find her room. Eventually, he found a room with an Aboriginal woman sleeping in it. In the next room, there she was. He was beginning to wonder how you could admire someone and at the same time despise them. It was all about those who were born into money and those that were just destined to survive. His brain wasn't big enough to accept that, yes, that was a definite advantage, but if you had it in you and some guts and determination, you could be anything you wanted in this country, even with physical disabilities. She looked so peaceful, lying there under the mosquito net, in her almost see-through lace nightie. But he wasn't here for sex; he was here to kill. *Jessy's death was an accident*, he said to himself, but he knew Maxine was to blame for the position he was in now.

Bunya, Maxine's Aboriginal maid, was very protective and fussed over her. She was awake, listening to the sounds of silence, when she thought she heard a noise. Then nothing.

I must have imagined it, she thought. *No, wait, there it is again, like something being squeezed or pushed.*

All the wooden window panels were held open on their stick supports. She looked out her window and saw someone climbing in Maxine's window.

She screamed, 'Hey, you, what are you doing? Get out of there. Maxine, Maxine, look out! Help, someone, help!'

When help arrived, she said, 'When I screamed, he jumped back out of the window and ran off in the dark.'

'What did he look like? Did you recognise him?'

'Yes, it was the Bunyip! He was covered in lots and lots of hair. I could only see his beady little eyes when he looked at me. When I was little, the elders of our tribe said he had lived out here for hundreds of years, and now I have seen him. The Bunyip can turn itself into anything it wants, man or beast, trees or a bird, my father said.'

Suddenly, the night sky lit up as the above ground fuel tanks exploded. While everyone was distracted by the fire, the Bunyip Man made his escape.

I'll get her next time, he thought, *and that black girl as well.*

CHAPTER SEVENTEEN

Matilda said, 'The underground tanks of diesel, unleaded and avgas for the choppers will hold us for a month. The whole thing is really just a pain in the arse and another trip out here, that we didn't need, for the police to deal with this mystic Bunyip Man, which of course is a lot of frog shit.'

'There are a lot of unexplainable incidents that happen in the outback,' Maxine said, 'but this story of a Bunyip Man isn't one of them.'

It would be more than a week before new tanks and hoses could be sent out and the station workers build new platforms for the tanks. Only then could the road tanker start its journey to the station to fill the new tanks. Double Diamond, like most cattle stations in the outback, had reserves of most of the necessities to keep it rolling along.

* * *

The police air wing was to get the new Pilatus PC-24 jet, a twin engine jet that would cut travel times in half and ensure the quickest response times into the outback. It could carry eight officers or be configured to carry cargo and emergency equipment. It wouldn't be in police service till sometime in 2026, but Riley had been sent to Western Australia along with a select few for flight training with the aircraft and accreditation certificates to fly the aircraft when it was brought into service with PolAir.

Unfortunately, that was the time Ben and Clara had set for their wedding, so Riley wasn't there to see Maxine, or Feathers who had been asked to give the bride away. Maxine was bitterly disappointed that, once again, an opportunity to see him had been missed. There were many times she had to talk herself out of going to see him wherever he was, but it was important that she wasn't seen as pushing a one-sided love affair, thereby widening the gap between them, a gap she hoped was measured in kilometres and not feelings.

Clara and Ben had talked about visiting Double Diamond for some time so they went there soon after they were married. As the plane came down over the red dirt runaway and its wheels touched down and sent the red dust clouding into the air behind its wheels, Ben said, 'I am so excited! I've been looking forward to this for a long time. I can't believe we have arrived. The station looked fantastic from the air. What are all those large mounds spread out throughout the area?'

Clara said, 'They are magnetic termite mounds. Some can be as tall as two metres, built over a hundred years. Each mound has a queen termite who lives for the same time as the mound lasts for. They are called magnetic because they build their mounds in a consistent north-south direction, similar to how a compass needle points. This orientation helps to control the temperature and moisture required for their survival.'

A red dust cloud was heading their way. Hidden within it was a small Suzuki four-wheel drive with the top cut off and no doors, driven by Maxine.

'Jump in, you city slickers, and welcome to Double Diamond! The homestead staff who are old enough to know you are excited to see you. They have fixed up Mum and Dad's old room for you both, as they said you deserve the best room in the house. Tomorrow, due to the early muster start, I have arranged an early breakfast barbecue for managerial staff and those who matter in the decisions of the station contract to meet the other, "phantom" owner of the station. Tonight, in the bullpit room and bar, we will discuss the ever-increasing changes required for moving forward as a continued financially rewarding cattle station.'

'This place is fantastic,' Ben said. 'When do I get to ride a horse?'

'Whoa there, steady, partner. You'll have a sore cowboy arse before you leave here. There is a muster on tomorrow; only two hundred cattle to bring in this time, mainly for health checks. And you, my brother in-law, can ride a horse on the muster all day tomorrow and the next day while my sister and I get re-acquainted. We'll have the liniment rub ready for you each night.'

Getting reacquainted, and knowing how her sister felt about Riley, Clara now finally realised that the early puppy love had not only gone away but had grown into something that could be a wonderful experience or an end-of-life disaster. And it seemed that Maxine was prepared to take the chance, although she didn't know the why. Clara said to herself, *What can I do? Sometimes love is blind and other times so precious.* She dared not interfere. It would have to play itself out.

That evening, Maxine opened the meeting, thanked them all for their attendance and introduced her sister co-owner. It was obvious that Maxine was the one in the family to have the say where the station was concerned.

'As you would know, we are well into 2019, which has seen significant changes to our industry, particularly here in the outback. The drought here has impacted our cattle. We will need to destock by selling some of our breeding cows for slaughter. This reduction in the herd will be the loss of valuable genetics, the loss of our parents' generations of breeding, which will impact the diversity of the herd. It will be difficult to find breeding cattle to rebuild the herd, as I suspect other stations will have had to do what we will have to do.'

Clara said, 'is it that bad?

'I'm afraid so,' said Matilda. 'If we don't take some action, we will go down.'

CHAPTER EIGHTEEN

Matilda gave Ben the mildest mannered, trained stock horse the station had, one they kept for important visitors who wanted to be part of it all. The station hands helped Ben up on the horse, who was called Rosemary. She had seen her day and usually spent it resting in the long paddock; that is, the homestead grass and garden area. But she would be as kind and gentle as she could be for this city slicker who wasn't rough and nasty to her but had no idea about a horse. She let him think he was an expert in telling her what to do and where to go after a stray cow. Dr Ben Forrester looked ridiculously out of place straddling Rosemary. She did all the moves and positioning that was required during a muster, and she had made the city dude look good, but despite all her efforts, he fell off anyway.

The muster was in full swing. The cattle were being separated by breed and sex into separate yards, the cows chosen for the saleyards put to one side. As the station's vet, Maxine inspected the animals for disease or pregnancy.

When the dust of the muster had settled and the choppers had landed, the station hands helped Ben off the horse, and as he walked bow-legged towards the homestead, he looked like he had shat in his pants.

They gave him a round of applause and called out, 'See you tomorrow same time, mate. We'll have Rosemary ready for you.'

'Smartarses,' he said under his breath.

When the girls saw him, they couldn't stop laughing, and Bunya had to leave the room so they didn't see her grinning. When it was time for bed, he had to sleep on his stomach after Clara had massaged his bum with liniment. To add insult to injury, it was horse liniment. Day two of the muster saw Ben standing in the back of one of the utes for the day. They all gave him recognition for determination and being a good bloke.

* * *

The Aboriginal youth from the gang who had escaped had been working his way slowly along the dry creek bed when he stumbled onto the small cave dug into the side of the riverbed. Inside were the three girls, terrified it was the Bunyip Man.

'What the hell!' he said as he took off their gags.

'Quick! Get us out of here before the Bunyip Man comes back.'

As they headed off down the creek bed, they could hear a motorcycle coming in the distance.

The Bunyip Man had been living in the outback for years. His hair was matted and filthy and had grown down to his waist and over his face, of which all you could were two small eyes. What was left of his clothes were tied together with bits or hay bale twine, and his shoes had worn down into a weird looking sandal held on his feet by string stolen from various farms. His small frame was hunchbacked. He frightened the hell out of the local Aboriginals, and they spread the stories and sighting of him far and wide. He was now like the real Bunyip Man according to ancient Aboriginal mythology. Some of the tribes left food out for him in the hope that he would take the food offered and not harm them. His brain over the years had been boiled in the hot sun of the outback and he was now anything but a normal human being. He had become a dangerous animal. And he had a dozen hiding places if he heard an aircraft.

The girls and the boy were seen by the station's workers checking the bores, wells and fences, who couldn't believe what the girls told them. As it was a four-hour drive to take them to the police in Tennant Creek and then a six-hour drive back to the station, they decided to take them straight to the station with them, which was only two hours, where the police could get them. The boy went his own way back to his tribe.

Once the girls had told their stories, had showered and been given clean clothes, they were given medical checks by Clara. They were all okay and hadn't been touched. The police were on their way and the white girl's parents were notified by radio; the police would deliver the Aboriginal girls back to their village. The police and the girls stayed overnight and flew out the next morning.

The rest of the week was spent showing Ben around Double Diamond and outlying areas.

CHAPTER NINETEEN

The vegetation on the outskirts of the cattle station was mainly hummock grasslands dominated by diverse species of spinifex long grass, and the occasional upside-down boab tree, with its branches buried in the earth and its roots reaching for the sky. Its bulbous trunk can hold thousands of litres of water to see it through the dry season and the Indigenous people discovered how to extract the water for their own use.

Hidden in this vegetation was the Bunyip Man, waiting for the cover of night to exact his revenge on what his brain conceived as the select few. When night came, it brought with it a moon that hung low over the outback landscape, and created a sense of mystery, and under a canopy of stars that seemed to stretch to infinity, he slowly crept into the main working and storage sheds of the station, far enough away from the homestead not to be seen. He was carrying a small container of red sandy soil, and a ten-litre empty can to steal fuel for the motorcycle. He entered the shed with the aircraft, poured the sand into their three fuel tanks and disappeared back into the night. The sand particles would settle in the bottom of the aircraft tanks and eventually would be sucked up into fuel line, clogging the fuel filter and fuel lines and damaging the fuel pump and injectors, leading to engine shut down and fatal consequences.

At that same moment, Matilda had just completed his rounds of security before retiring for the night. *What was that?* he said to himself. 'Who's there?' he called out. He circled around the sheds but found nothing. *Maybe I imagined it. We are all spooked after the last episode,* he thought before he headed off to bed.

It was an early start the next morning. The cattle were still being sorted and inspected. Arrangements had been made for Ben to go up in one of the choppers the next day when they looked for stray or missed cattle, and Ben was excited about his first ever helicopter flight. Matilda was in the sorting yard with the cattle, but couldn't get last night off his mind. He hadn't found anything or anyone, but after what had previously happened, he was ...

Jesus, the aircraft shed! That's where I thought I heard someone.

He jumped over the stockyard rails and ran for the sheds, but he was too late. The chopper with Ben had lifted off and banked away. He was in time to alert the second one not to go until it was checked, which would take time. Yet, maybe this was all for nothing. Maybe he was just being paranoid.

The station radioed the chopper and suggested, under the circumstances, they turn back. The pilot said everything was running normally – the pressure, temperature and engine revs were all normal – but thanks for the warning, and he would keep an eye on his gauges.

They were a hundred and sixty-four kilometres out from the station according to their positioning device, hovering over the top of three stray cows and trying to push them out of the dry creek bed at Lizard Junction. They had just banked away to get some height to come back for another push. The alarm came on loudly – *whoop, whoop, whoop* – and down they went nose first into the creek bed's steep bank, shattering the poly glass cockpit bubble, with the rotor blades stuck deep into the creek's soft bank.

The pilot's head was crushed into the instrument panel because he was in the habit of never wearing his seat harness. Ben was wearing his, but his legs were crushed under the collapsed front nose of the helicopter. He lost consciousness several times. When he came to, he heard the station calling.

He grabbed the microphone and said, 'We are down. Pilot dead. My legs crushed in the wreckage. Need help asap.'

'Can you reach the green button that says BA?'

'Yes.'

'Press that button. That is the beacon activation, and we will find you.'

But there was nowhere for a fixed wing Flying Doctor to land. A military medivac helicopter was activated along with a police helicopter rescue team. He was stabilised and flown to Royal Darwin Hospital. His left leg had to be amputated above the knee. Which at least would make it easier to walk with his artificial limb because he still had his own knee joints.

The devastating news of the crash had reached the station, and Clara was on her way to Darwin.

'At least he is alive,' Maxine said.

Matilda was beside himself and handed in his resignation.

'We are not accepting it, Matilda. It's not your fault. You must not feel guilty. The police will get this bastard. In the meantime, we ae going to have to strengthen our security, and I need you looking after that for us. So, please, let's not hear any more talk of resignation. You are an important part of the successful running of this station, particularly when I'm not here.'

Maxine was away now a lot of the time visiting properties as the vet. Most of her days were spent driving the long distances between them, and in some cases, she stayed overnight.

In the hanger next to the two helicopters was the station's fixed wing 150 Cessna, and although it had not been used since Spencer had passed away, it had been kept in pristine condition.

Maxine thought, '*I really must get my licence to fly. This is a perfectly good airplane that is doing nothing that should be brought back in service, particularly with me in it, and written on the side will be "Australian Outback Veterinarian".*'

CHAPTER TWENTY

Riley was on the morning shift and took the call from Bazza.

'Ben's been in a helicopter accident at Double Diamond,' he said. 'He will have his left leg amputated above the knee.'

'What the hell happened?'

'The chopper was sabotaged with sand in the tank by someone there called the Bunyip Man. Who the hell is that?'

'No such person. It's an Aboriginal myth. But they will get whoever it is.'

Bazza said he was on his way to Darwin to see Ben, and that this story and others about the Double Diamond cattle station had been spread throughout the force.

'What sort of stories?' said Riley.

'Stories that it's not a good safe place to go. People who go there are never seen again. They just disappear or are found dead.'

'Look, I haven't been there for many years, but I've never heard so much bullshit. You know what happens, Bazza. The more times a story is told the more exaggerated it gets, and it gets out of hand. I suspect that's what's happening here.'

'Well, it's become the "infamous" Double Diamond cattle station,' Bazza said. 'Apparently, the amount of times the police have to travel there is not normal. Anyway, I'm just giving you a head up as a mate on the talk among the police and the authorities in the outback system.'

* * *

Ben stayed with his parents in Brisbane to convalesce while his new wife Clara had to return to work. She came back on the weekends to help him wobble along on his new leg. He was getting good at it and would soon be back at the hospital with the sick kids. Clara was at the woman's clinic at the same hospital, and the way his progress was going, things would soon be back to normal, meaning they'd be together again. Riley sent his best wishes and a "get well soon" message.

Wednesday, 14 September 2021 was Riley's fortieth birthday. He had been invited to an evening meal at the La Vue Waterfront French restaurant in Brisbane with Bazza, Ben and Clara. They opened a bottle of Wynns $250 Black Label Cabernet Sauvignon to celebrate Riley and Ben's marvellous recovery.

'Here, here!' they all said.

'Well, make the most of this,' said Bazza. 'You doctors might be able to afford this; Riley and I are only bloody public servants.'

Riley had duck risotto, a veal eye fillet and a chocolate parfait. Bazza had king prawns, the lamb and rosemary jus and and the crumble. Clara had the *foie gras*, ocean trout and profiteroles. And Ben had the pork belly, tiger prawns thermidor and an affogato. They spent the rest of the evening with casual banter about any future family plans that Ben and Clara might have and what the cattle station's long-term plans might be as far as the family ownership was concerned.

Clara said, 'Well, any future plans regarding Double Diamond would certainly be what Maxine decides. She is the expert where the station's future might lie, and I would be one hundred per cent with what her decision might be. And while we are talking about Maxine, Riley, you are such a bone head! All these years, Maxine has worshipped the ground you walk on. She has loved you without exception from the time she was a little girl and said to you, "I really like you, Riley". You told her you would go back to see how beautiful she had grown. You obviously don't realise she has waited and watched each day for you all these years. She looks up that red dirt track from the homestead every day, with hope in her heart. She was thirty last month and she's not getting any younger. I haven't interfered and said anything before, but it is well past the time you were told. The woman loves you and adores you. You need to do something about it, one way or the other, you dumb bastard!

*   *   *

The search continued for the motorcycle monster. He had the cunning of a fox. Air and ground searches had failed to find him. Stories were told within the Aboriginal camps about this dreaded killer monster that could turn himself into a motorcycle, a tree or a rocks, and it was said he had been seen turning himself into a kangaroo. They had seen him in the shadows behind a tree, or maybe he was the tree; they were never sure. He had also been seen as far away as Coober Pedy and Mount Isa. The stories about this mythical man went through the outback towns like wildfire. Anything that happened that was bad, or if someone was found dead, it was blamed on the monster man.

*　*　*

Maxine was back at the station from her vet travels in September. She had turned thirty a couple of weeks ago and was now at the age where she considered birthdays as just another day older than yesterday. The Double Diamond weather was now shifting towards the dry season and ongoing mustering activities. Once again, the yard work of weaning the calves from their mothers and separating for branding, ear tagging and vaccinating would be done. They drafted and sorted weaned cattle based on age, sex and intended use, for example, breeders, heifers not for breeding and male weaners. Then there was the outrider or bore workers' responsibility of checking the wells, pumps, stray cattle, fences and windmills, building repairs, vehicle and aircraft maintenance.

'... and the list just goes on and on, and eventually in time it will all repeat itself,' said Maxine, as she had a sly glance down through the pepper gum trees to the red dirt track that led from the station to infinity, and the red dirt air strip that ran along the side. *It all looks abandoned and forlorn*, Maxine thought. It all seemed to be saying, 'I'm lonely out here by myself. Someone, come and provide some activity.'

Where are you, Riley? Will you come back?

She quickly chastised herself for getting sentimental. She had one last look, then turned away.

CHAPTER TWENTY-ONE

There was a huge police parade in March to be held in Sydney, and Riley and Bazza had been given approval to attend, so they would travel down together.

The police band led more than three hundred police officers on motorcycles, horseback and on foot through the streets of Sydney to the police shrine of remembrance for fallen comrades. Large crowds gathered on each side of the road and showed their appreciation and support as they marched past. Riley and Bazza stood in the outside row of the group. At the police shrine's assembly point, the commissioner spoke followed by the prime minister.

Bang! Bang! Bang!

Three shots rang out. The officer next to Riley went down, and so did Bazza. Riley saw where the flash had come from and took off in that direction. The shooter went behind the memorial wall with Riley in hot pursuit. The shooter was the brother of a man the police had shot and killed during a bank robbery. He was now hiding in waiting for Riley to appear. Riley came bursting around the corner. He was shot in the stomach and fell almost at the feet of the shooter.

The shooter looked at Riley and said, 'You pig! Now you pay for my brother's killing.'

He pointed the gun at Riley, who closed his eyes and waited. A police motorcyclist came, seemingly from nowhere, and shot the shooter in the head. The motorcycle cop came over and knelt down.

'Riley, you're an idiot!'

He took off his police helmet.

Riley said, 'Toby, for Christ's sake! It *is* you. What a coincidence! I am in your debt, mate. How can I ever thank you?'

'You look pretty well shot up, so shut up. The ambulance is on the way. You and Bazza will be travelling together, by the look of it. Don't you die on me, you bastard – you owe me dinner.'

Clara and Ben flew down to be with his father. Bazza had been hit in the right side of his chest. The doctor told them it was quite high so he would make a full recovery.

'What about Riley?'

'Well, he is a very sick man. He was hit in the stomach and has some internal organ damage. The bullet has torn blood vessels and there has been significant internal bleeding. Part of his intestines and liver have been perforated by the bullet. We need to control any intestinal spillage into his abdominal cavity that could cause infection and inflammation, which can lead to sepsis, which is life threatening. He has just come from the operating theatre, so now it's all up to him if he survives.'

'He is a fighter.'

'I hope you're right, because he will need to be if he is to survive.'

Clara said, 'What do I do, Ben? Do I tell my sister or not?'

'It might be best to wait to see what the outcome is first.'

'And if he dies and she had a chance to see him? She will never talk to me again.'

'Well, he's unconscious so she couldn't talk to him at the moment, and nobody is allowed in to visit him, so we should wait and not tell her just yet.'

Several days later, Riley regained consciousness and asked Clara not to tell Maxine. He didn't want her worrying. He would tell her himself when he thought the time was right. She was glad they hadn't said anything to Maxine, and now she had an excuse.

* * *

Double Diamond and all other properties north of Tennant Creek had received the warning of a large storm coming their way, which often happened when the dry season got closer. They had been preparing for it for the last two days, although these outback storms had a way of showing little respect for any preparations that were made. A flock of black kites hovered lazily above, watching for their prey of lizards, small mammals and insects that would be available after the storm and the rain.

Suddenly the darkness came, with the arrival of bolts of white lightning that could stop and restart a thousand hearts heralding the sound of nature's drums in the sky. Whip cracking its blinding light through the dark heavens, the storm grew stronger, with the wind unaware of its own strength, smashing and destroying everything in its path. Flying sheets of iron and timber like missiles were lost in the thick clouds of red dust and anything that wasn't tied down or solid was blown down like a stack of dominoes. Animals and stock cringed and leant into each other against the wind.

The stillness as the eye of the storm came through was a short space of time to check on damage, injuries and stock. Then came the storm's companion. The sky opened, and a deluge of heavy rain came down vertically in a veil of sharp thin pieces of steel, slicing into dams and wells, hammering, lashing and battering the now saturated and waterlogged ground. Thunder rumbled and crackled somewhere in the heavens. Then like magic, the wind was gone, and the pelting rain began to fall softly like petals, making circles in the pools of ground water. The storm was gone as quickly as it had arrived, and left behind it a damp, silent and eerie feeling.

Maxine was concerned about the horses, but she had sent the two young stable hands in with the horses to try and pacify them during the storm. When she arrived, the stables had been extensively damaged, and two horses had minor injuries. Jed had kicked his stable door down but looked all right. One of the young stable boys had a broken arm, and both of them had wet their pants. Maxine and Matilda did the rounds of the station, making a list of supplies needed to replace or repair the storm damage. Luckily, the storm hadn't lasted long enough to do serious damage or injure the cattle.

For some reason now, she was lonely, more so than she had ever been. He had said he would, he promised he would, but he wasn't coming back, was he? Why would he come back to the middle of nowhere? He was a senior pilot in the police air wing, with access to fancy restaurants, dinner cruises on the Brisbane River and an abundance of women to choose from. She had tried on many occasions to remove him from her mind; he just wouldn't leave. She had written to him on several occasions, letters straight from her heart. But she had never posted them; they were in her bedside drawer tied with a pink ribbon.

She decided that, while the storm repairs which she wasn't involved in were the priority at the moment, and the dry season had now begun, she would clear out and do a boundary fence ride. She hooked up the horse float to Land

Cruiser number one and loaded Jed and her supplies. She told Matilda and Bunya she would be back in three days.

Maxine drove out to the closest corner boundary fence called Cassowary Corner, about one hundred and thirty kilometres out from the station, unloaded the horse, packed her swag, rifle and a few supplies and headed off on her beloved Arabian stallion. There was a group of ten or so cattle slowly wandering towards the station. If they were still there when she came back, she would push them along further towards the station, but for now they would be fine. She rode along casually, letting the horse cool his legs in the shallow water as they went. Lizard Creek would soon be just a dry gully; the trickle of water there would soon dry up.

Her mind was miles away. She hadn't heard from Clara for quite some time and a woman's intuition kept telling her that something was wrong. She didn't see the inland taipan, but the horse did and reared on its hind legs, throwing Maxine into the middle of a large tangle of barbed wire that had been washed downstream in the last wet season. Jed had gone. She was sure he would go back to the station, and someone would come looking for her. Meantime, hopelessly tangled in the barbed wire, she needed to try and keep still. Every time she moved, the barbed wire cut into her. They weren't expecting her back for another two days, and if the horse didn't go back at all, she was definitely going to be stuck for the next two days and nights. She tried desperately to free herself, but she was hopelessly stuck and all she did was cut herself more.

She now started to come to terms with the thought of all night in the barbed wire, and where that bloody snake might have crawled to. Her mind started to race to things like wild pigs that could rip you to pieces with their tusks, and a nest of giant bull ants that could be near or under her, starving wild dogs, foxes and dingoes roaming the outback ... she would be at their mercy. All through the night, whenever she thought she heard something, she would call out loudly, 'Get away, get away,' just in case something was there.

She heard a motorcycle coming in the distance. Just as she thought she was safe, he appeared – the Bunyip Man. She could smell him from where he stood, his whole body covered in long hair and, like the stories told, two beady little eyes among the thick facial hair.

His small, bent body shook when a voice from somewhere in among the hair said, 'Well, look who we have here, all parcelled up ready for the picking.'

He pigeon-toed over to the barbed wire entanglement and poked his hand in through a small gap. He had very long fingernails and there were small black things alive and moving under the nails. He touched her on the leg and she kicked out at him. He cut his hand on the barbed wire and swore.

'You bitch! You won't be so smart when I get you out of there and get through with you.'

He had nothing to cut the wire with and each time he handled the wire, he was cut. He tried ramming the motorcycle into the coils of wire, which only made it worse. Both his hands were bleeding badly now.

He sat down to think about what to do next, and how to get into her.

* * *

'Mr Matilda, Mr Matilda,' Bunya said, 'Jed has come back without Maxine. Something bad has obviously happened.'

'Get that chopper ready to go, he said to one of the pilots.'

'I'm coming with you.'

They took off and banked away, following the track they knew she would have taken. It wasn't long before they found the Land Cruiser. They could see she had taken her bed roll and overnight gear.

'This is where she left on the horse', said Matilda.

They lifted off again to search.

*   *   *

The Bunyip Man had managed to get halfway into the barbed wire coil. His hands and arms were torn to shreds and bleeding.

'I'm coming for you, you bitch,' he kept repeating.

Maxine kicked and spat at him, telling him he was a filthy swine and that she would kill him if he touched her. Suddenly the echoing thump, thump of helicopter blades beating the air was heard coming along the gully.

Maxine said, 'Here they come, and you, you bastard, are dead.'

He tore himself free from the wire just as the chopper came round the bend. He made a break for the motorcycle. Matilda opened fire. The Bunyip Man was hit several times as he staggered to the bike, but when they swung around and landed, he was gone. But he had left a blood trail behind him.

'He will probably die somewhere out there in no man's land——' they said.

'——and his carcass eaten by predators, and good riddance,' Maxine said.

'I would've liked to have seen the proof of a body,' said Matilda.

They cut Maxine out of the wire and called another chopper to get Matilda back to the Land Cruiser while Maxine was flown to the station. As luck sometimes happens, the Flying Doctor had come out to the station for the children's immunisation program, so the nurse dressed Maxine's wounds, and she was given a tetanus shot. Her next stop was to see her beloved horse and reward it with a carrot for raising the alarm.

She said to the young stable boy, 'You make sure he gets a really good rub down.'

'Yes, ma'am!'

* * *

Riley was out of intensive care and off the danger list. He had received notification that he had been reassigned as the senior pilot to the Alice Spring police air wing. He checked their inventory of aircraft as a matter of interest. There were two Pilatus PC 12 fixed wing aircraft, and a Bell 206 JetRanger helicopter, and eight pilots. *All that will suit me just fine*, he said to himself. He also knew that Alice was only five hundred kilometres from Tennant Creek, and he knew what else was nearby.

The air wing covered a vast area of the Northern Territory, not only Tennant Creek located in the Barkly Tablelands region, but several other small towns along the Stuart Highway between Alice and Darwin like Wycliffe, Barrow Creek, Newcastle Waters, Banka Banka, Daly Waters, Mataranka and Renner Springs, along with outlying cattle stations including the Double Diamond. The Alice air wing had a huge area of responsibility, and he was looking forward to being part of it.

The Australia-wide police air wing was a close-knit mob,

and from different detachments, seminars and training courses, most pilots knew each other. When he arrived, they couldn't wait to give him all the stories about the Bunyip Man and the stories that had grown out of hand about the Double Diamond cattle station. Nobody knew that he had been born on the station, and he decided nobody needed to know, not right now anyway. There were jokes and cartoon drawings of what some comedians thought the Bunyip Man looked like, and an aerial photo of the Double Diamond cattle station and its surroundings. He asked them about the photo. They said it was to do with the search for the Bunyip Man at the station some time ago, and recently out at Lizard Creek, one of the owners, a thirty-year old-woman called Maxine Roper had been involved in an incident with him a hundred or so kilometres out into the property.

'What sort of an incident?' Riley asked.

They gave him the case file to read.

Riley managed to chase down Feathers, his old friend and muster pilot. They were having a meal and drinks by the pool at the Barra and Todd Restaurant and Bar, on the other side of the dry Todd River from the town.

'I suppose you've been given all the gossip, rumours, Aboriginal stories and myths now surrounding the Double Diamond,' Feathers said.

Riley said, 'Yes and I've read the police report they have called "Red Dust and Barbed Wire".'

'I don't know all the facts, but it must have been horrendous for Maxine. The problem now is the locals and Indigenous community have turned a murdering animal, who could be still out there somewhere, into some sort of folklore mystery Bunyip, of which there is no such thing. But this person, whoever he is, definitely real.'

CHAPTER TWENTY-TWO

He was on the bones of his arse and had been living on a day-to-day basis for some time, getting nowhere. He was waiting for the message that the men had arrived in Australia. He had no idea who they were or what they would be doing, but the money he would get for helping them would be significant. The money the Tennant Creek gold mine paid while he waited was a mere pittance to what the mine made, and it was time he rectified that and made it an even playing field, particularly where he was concerned.

His name was Zachery, Zach for short. He was very fit for his thirty years of hard physical labour, but time was running out for how much longer he could keep that up. He didn't want a handout; he wanted a hand up but hadn't managed that from anyone. Though he was very good at making things from metal – he made small metal model windmills and sold them at the Mindil Beach Sunset Market in Darwin – sometimes he would sell a couple and other times none. He couldn't survive like that. He needed a steady income, so he'd moved down to Tennant Creek and started work with the gold mine. He paid rent for a small bedsitter at the back of a shop. His only possession was an old ex-army Series 1 Land Rover with pieces of black scrap metal left over from making the windmills scattered in the back, an old canvas tent with some camping stuff and the clothes he had on his back, just the bare minimum to survive.

His positions at the mine varied from week to week. One week he would be working in the extraction section, where the crushing of the ore occurred to extract the gold, or where the refining was done to remove impurities. On other days, he would work in the melting and casting section where the gold was melted and poured into moulds to form bars of varying sizes. And lately, he had worked with the finishing process where cooling, polishing and stamping occurred. He would wait till next he worked in the finishing section and they were pouring one-kilogram bars and steal two of them before they were counted and stamped. He thought a one kilogram bar of gold was worth $170,000. $340,000 would do him nicely; he wasn't greedy.

He waited as long as he could for the men he was to help. His plan was to get to one of the outback stations and become part of the workforce, hide there until the heat was off, during which time he would have found a buyer. He was prepared to sell them for $300,000, $40,000 under market value.

*   *   *

The police air wing in Darwin was down two pilots, so Alice Springs had been asked to provide two on loan for a short time till they were replaced through the system. Riley and one other were selected because they were single. Rather than send a man away from his family, it was always a single pilot who did detachments as there was no indication as to how long the detachment might be. Riley smiled, packed his gear into his Land Cruiser and headed for Darwin, stopping at Katherine overnight. Once he arrived, he would be slotted into the rostered pilot's shiftwork and other duties involving aircraft movement and maintenance.

Riley now held the rank of Senior Sergeant. The rank of pilots in the police air wing was determined by their progress within the general police force structure, not by their role as a pilot. The police union had long ago stopped the force using pilots for general duties other than those related to air support. Riley remembered when Clara first asked about rank structure for police pilots, she was flabbergasted.

'So, let's get this straight. If two new officers start and one is a pilot and the other just general duties, they are both just constables. There is no acknowledgment for the experience and expertise and qualifications required of the pilot. That bloody stinks!'

'We do receive a higher wage and other benefits that the same rank doesn't get.'

'And so you bloody should! In all other government bodies like the military, all their pilots are officers, not bloody privates, and work their way up. Bloody pathetic! They have already admitted it is a separate section of the force, as in the air wing, and it requires its own aviation rank structure, for example, Flying Officer Riley or Senior Flight Officer Riley.'

Riley wasn't big on rank – he just wanted to fly – but she was probably right in what she said. He would do what he normally did, and just fit in.

*　*　*

The workers had lined up at the mine to get their allocated work areas for the week. When it was Zach's turn, the foreman called out, 'You're in the finishing shed this week, Zach.'

The finishing shed had a corrugated iron roof and sides that only went halfway down to the ground in an attempt to get a breeze through. The smelting area was hot, and the heat often wafted through to the finishing area.

Zach had given much thought to getting away with the gold bars. He would steal them on Thursday by throwing them out under the side wall into the long grass, then come back at night to get them. He waited till there were thirty-three bars lined up ready for polishing. When the smoko whistle blew and the others left, he threw two of them out into the long grass. When the workers came back, he was careful who he picked to witness the count, someone who wasn't the sharpest tool in the shed. He quickly shuffled the gold bars around like cards as he counted them. The count was verified by the other worker. The foreman came with the lock and combination for the safe. He was supposed to also check the count to verify the bars were all there. He had done this count so many times in the past that it had become a pain in the arse. The count was always correct, and who the hell would try and steal the gold bars? It was never going to happen, so sometimes he didn't bother counting, like this time.

Zach had it all under control. He retrieved the gold bars that night, painted them black and buried them among the black metal scraps in the back of his Land Rover. The next morning when the safe was opened, Zach told the foreman there were two bars missing from yesterday's count.

'Don't give me that,' he said, and he did what he should have done the day before and counted them. 'Jesus, the shit is going to hit the fan! Nobody go anywhere!'

Management came and did their own count and spoke to the workers. Zach was covered. He had the foreman as a witness who had to agree they were all there yesterday when they went into the safe. The foreman couldn't admit he hadn't counted them. Nobody saw Zach smiling. The local police arrived along with detectives from Alice Springs and Darwin. Everyone's vehicle was impounded at the mine that day, and along with the owner of the vehicle, was searched. When the detective got to Zach's old Land Rover, the detective was more interested in the old model vehicle than anything else. He searched the front under the seats and under the dashboard. He looked in the back among the old buggered tent and camping gear.

'What's all those bits of metal for?'

Zach showed him some photos of the small windmills he made as a hobby and explained the metal were the offcuts.

'I wouldn't mind getting one for the police station,' he said. 'In the main entrance, the ladies have made a small indoor garden and fernery. A small windmill like that would look great in among the ferns. When you make some more, let me know.'

Zach promised him if he made another one, it would be his. The detective went with Zach and searched his bedsitter at the back of the shop.

'Okay, you can go, but don't leave town. If you do, we need to know where you are going.'

'I'll be just going out camping,' Zach said.

'No worries. Keep in touch with us.'

The police, mine managers and owners were at a loss. They had the word of the foreman, a long time employee, that all the bars were in the safe the night before. They also had two employees who said the count was correct when the gold bars went into the safe, seen by three witnesses.

The senior detective said, 'That being the case, it just leaves the answer to who had the combination to the safe. There were three of them. The owner, the manager, and the foreman, and since the foreman has his alibi and witnesses, and it is unlikely to be the owner or the manager, who weren't even there at the time, it's obvious the initial count must have been wrong.'

Until any other facts were uncovered, the case was put to one side as an unsolved case due to lack of evidence or leads.

Zach checked with the foreman and said, 'I think, under the circumstances, I'll be giving notice till things sort themselves out.'

'Everyone will be under suspicion, but we have each other as witnesses that it wasn't us, so they can find some other fall guy,' the foreman said.

Zach took his few belongings from the bedsitter, bought some supplies and headed out.

CHAPTER TWENTY-THREE

Zach had a choice of three cattle stations to choose from. He chose Double Diamond because it was within the range of fuel he had, and he didn't want to be camping in the outback longer than necessary. He could take his time and spend a couple of days to travel the three hundred and something kilometres. There was no need to bring attention to himself.

Day one saw him a hundred and fifty kilometres in the barren outback, and without losing his way on the tracks and shallow river gully crossings, he was happy with where he was. He sat by his small fire that night as a small mob of Aboriginals arrived and set up nearby. They shared some of their local tucker with him: goanna, witchety grubs and nuts. He gave them some of his tucker: a can of food, a banana, a couple of camel sausages and a swig from the bottle of Scotch for the elders. They sat around the fire and told him the stories of the Bunyip Man and warned him to be on his guard when by himself, that every tree, wallaby or lizard could be the Bunyip, ready to take him away and devour him. They said he had a motorcycle that he could make disappear or reappear whenever he wanted.

The next day, Maxine saw a red dust cloud coming from a long way off. The station almost never had visitors or arrivals they weren't expecting, and just for a moment, her heart skipped a beat. The old Land Rover drove in under the stone archway and was joined by dogs barking, kids with runny noses and a pet calf. Matilda had also seen the vehicle coming and had joined the throng around the vehicle.

'Hello there,' he said to Zach. 'What brings you out here?'

'I'm looking for work.'

'What can you do?'

'I have worked on stations in Western Australia, and I'm fairly well experienced in most areas. I am good with my hands and have a good mechanical aptitude. I'm not a professional by any means, but I'd appreciate a job and somewhere to stay, or I could set up my old tent.'

'There's no need to do that. We will fit you in. We might even set you up as a bore runner.'

'That would suit me. I don't mind working by myself out in the open.'

'Come on down to the station office and we'll get your details. This is the main homestead area and it's out of bounds to station workers. There is a large machine shed down past the stockyards, and in there at one end, you will find the workers' cars parked where you can put yours. The shed helps to keep the red dust out of the cars' air filters and breathers.'

Maxine watched the stranger arrive and go off with Matilda. Just another casual worker, she decided, and she really didn't need to know the details.

CHAPTER TWENTY-FOUR

Zach began to relax. Everything seemed to be going to plan. They had given him a new Land Cruiser number four, with equipment, spare parts and stores. The other bore runner's Land Cruiser was number three. They were both fitted with long range radios and their call signs back to the station were Bravo Romeo 3 and 4. They had enough rations and stores for two weeks. Both bore runners would head out south-west and then split into their own mapped individual areas of bores, wells, dams, windmills and fences that needed maintenance. They would also have the usual responsibilities for checking the welfare of stray cattle and calves.

Zach's problem was what to do with the gold bars. Could he take the risk and leave them in his old Land Rover, or would he take them with him on the bore run? He decided to take make another windmill. Using the gold bars as a base, he glued them to a frame made from the offcuts using strong bonding epoxy glue. Then he sprayed the finished windmill and base black. He placed the windmill on the floor in the corner of his room. If the kids now pinched the bits of metal left in the old Land Rover, it didn't matter.

The first night out, the bore runners camped together before splitting and going their own ways in the morning. At that particular time of year in the outback, a canvas awning pulled out from the roof of the vehicle and pegged to the ground for some overhead cover of the swag was all that was required. Bore runners always carried a quantity of wood for a fire and resupplied it along the way wherever they could. The outback was bloody cold at night, and it helped keep some of the nasty night things that crawled, wriggled and flew at bay.

The bloke he was sharing the fire with called himself Dusty; his real name was Dustin. He had been on cattle stations all his life, and this was his sixteenth year as a bore runner at Double Diamond. They sat around the fire, and he gave Zach the history as he knew it about the movers and groovers that kept Double Diamond alive. He spoke about the Roper Family, particularly Spencer and Aileen, and the girls. He told Zach about the tragic circumstances of the oldest girl, Jessy, and a young boy named Riley who, he had to admit, he had a huge amount of time for. But he had been gone now for many years, and the old hands of the station knew that the youngest daughter, Maxine, had been heartbroken when Riley left to fly with the police. Maxine was now in her thirties and owned the station with her sister, Clara, who was a doctor, married in Queensland.

'There has been a lot of things happening out here, some of them unexplainable, and then there's been those that most of us have the answers to. But it's safer to just leave it alone.'

Zach said, 'So, tell me about this Bunyip thing.'

Dusty said, 'The word "Bunyip" is the Aboriginal term for what we would probably call a boogie man. Their Bunyip has been around in their folklore and mythology for hundreds of years. The one here they're calling the Bunyip is real, whatever or whoever it is, and is said to have been seen by several of the local inhabitants over the past several years. If he is still alive out here, he is damned dangerous. That's if it's a he – who knows what sex or sort of being it is? Occasionally, we find small calves have been cut up for their meat. It might be a couple of rogue blackfellows, or it could be this thing.'

Zach said, 'I don't understand why they haven't caught it. Look at this land he moves around in; it is as open as a possum sitting in a dead tree.'

Dusty said, 'Yes, you would think so, but this thing has been here for so long it could have built tunnels back to Tennant Creek by now, and it probably only moves around at night when it's cool. This thing, or person, must have hidden holes scattered throughout here. Mind you, it's not the bloody desert. Have a look out there. What do you see? Some boab trees, spinifex grass, love grass, sticky grass, Mitchel grass, and feather top grass. What grows where depends on whether it's that black clay or the red dirt your arse in on at the moment. Over to the left a way, there's those scraggy wattle species. So, while it's bloody barren, hot and unforgiving, it's hardly a desert.'

They packed their gear the next morning and said their goodbyes. There would now be at least a day's travel between them, but they would maintain radio contact between themselves and Double Diamond on a daily basis.

Zach arrived at his first bore hole. The aquifer beneath was a body of porous rock that held ground water and acted as a storage reservoir. Although the bores were part of the Great Artesian Basin, these ones didn't have the pressure to bring the flow naturally to the surface. They required a pump to extract the water from the aquifer. He changed the oil and spark plug, cleaned the filters, checked the pipes and connections to the well, checked the belts that drove the pump, reset the well float level, repaired the small, corrugated iron roof over the pump and wrote up the details in the service book with the time,

12.45 pm. When he arrived at bore well number two, it was 5.30. This site had a windmill to be maintained and serviced. He would be there all day tomorrow and maybe the next day as well, depending on what needed replacing or servicing.

'Bugger it,' he said, 'I'll set up camp and start tomorrow.'

He did his radio checks to the cattle station and called Dusty, got the fire going and set himself up for the night. He climbed into his bedroll next to the fire with the rifle by his side. His sleep was interrupted all night by the windmill's moaning and groaning and squeaking and creaking. He thought, *those bloody bearings will be getting covered in grease tomorrow, and whatever else is keeping me awake along with the rotating blades.*

The next morning, he climbed the ladder to where the main blades were slowly turning and squeaking. This windmill was a wind turbine for electricity generation. He watched as the wind flowed over the blades, creating lift and drag which caused the blades to spin. He saw the spinning blades were connected to a rotor, which was also rotating. The rotor was connected to a generator which converted the rotational motion to electrical energy that drove the pump to transfer water from the well. He replaced two bearings, repaired a blade, replaced the fuse to the main pump, left two spares and filled in the service sheet. As he left, he looked up at the big old windmill and smiled. There was another windmill worth $340,000 on the floor in his room back at the station.

Only forty kilometres away, he reckoned he would be at the next bore for lunch. The impression was that someone had said, 'Bugger it, just shove the thing here.' It was in the middle of nowhere and there was no shade. This one was a water pumping windmill. He looked up and saw the wind was causing the blades to rotate, same as the last one, but this one would have a gearbox and sucker rod. The rotating blades would be connected to a gearbox which transformed the energy to the up and down motion of a sucker rod. The sucker rod was connected to a plunger inside the well that pumped the water to the surface.

He checked its condition and what needed to be done, and it looked like he would be here for two days as well. When they did their radio checks, they decided to link up at the drovers hut the next day. It would give them a chance to swap some spare parts they both needed, and was a good excuse to have a bit of company and a yarn.

The drovers hut was initially built as a bore runner's emergency shelter during storms, but had also long ago been made available for the outback travelling public as a simple overnight accommodation stop. It was a one-room cabin with two wooden bunks, a small table and two rickety chairs, a fireplace with an old combustion stove and two small window openings with a wooden panel on a stick you could hold open to let in the breeze or drop down in the wet season to close the opening.

Outside the hut was a small artesian well, roughly circled with rocks with an overhead steel bar holding a rope and bucket to lower down to the pure clean drinking water. There was a notice board that said working bore runners had priority use of the hut. The facilities, plates, dishes, and utensils were to be left clean. Failure to look after the hut would see it closed to the travelling public.

As the hut came into view, he could see that Dusty's vehicle was already there, and smoke was coming from the chimney.

* * *

The Bunyip Man, who was in fact Steven Slowgo, or Bolta, who'd kidnapped Jessy all those years ago, was now stealing aviation gasoline from the forty-four gallon drums spread around throughout the outback for heli muster refuelling. He had discovered this large supply of one hundred per cent high octane fuel for his motorcycle, which meant his travel was unlimited to a large degree. He knew where the drovers hut was and had on other occasions spent time there. He was in fact on his way there now.

As he got closer, he saw the two bore runners' Land Cruisers at the hut. *So, two to one*, he said to himself. Would he come back when they were gone, or would he kill them both now? He needed to be careful. He didn't want the military out here looking for him. He would wait till dark and think about his next move.

CHAPTER TWENTY-FIVE

Riley had now been in Darwin for six months. He had enquired several times about when the replacement might be sent so he could return to Alice Springs. Nobody seemed to want to know. He was well liked by all, and being a Senior Sergeant, he was given the easy no-stress flying tasks, like flying high profile visitors around the state.

Meetings between government officials and local Tiwi Island councils in the past had achieved very little, so it was said the next meeting would be the most important. Three government officials from the Northern Territory Legislative Council and a Canberra representative would meet with the Tiwi Islands Land Council, the Regional Council and the Island Local Government representatives on the island.

The Tiwi Islands include Bathurst Island and Melville, about eighty kilometres from Darwin. The Tiwi people are an Indigenous Australian group who have lived on these islands for thousands of years. They are culturally different from groups on the mainland and have their own distinct language and unique customs, art and spiritual rituals.

Due to the nature of the meeting and the high-profile passengers, the police air wing had been tasked with the operation, which meant Riley would be flying to the Tiwi Islands with four passengers. It was only eighty kilometres away, so he wouldn't have a copilot. Considering the Pilatus

P12 has a cruising speed of five hundred and twenty-eight kilometres per hour, it could cover that distance in nine minutes. However, from runway to runway, it would be thirty minutes in actual time.

On Monday morning, Riley had done all his external flights checks and was waiting at the aircraft for the passengers to arrive.

Here they come, he said to himself. *Look at them. Bloody politicians, full of their own piss and importance, operating on the pretence that bullshit baffles brains. Still, I'll only have them for thirty minutes each way.*

He smiled and said, 'Good morning, I'm Senior Sergeant Riley, your pilot.'

The two women and two men smiled and boarded. One of the women asked if she could fly with him in the cockpit. She wanted to see how a plane was flown. Maybe he had judged her too quickly. She sat in the copilot's seat, on the right-hand side.

He made the announcement: 'Fasten your seat belts and enjoy the short thirty-minute flight.'

Riley pointed to the windsock. 'We will take off into the wind to the east and bank around to the north out to the island. See those two pedals down there? They will steer the plane round onto that east–west runway over there. Do you think you could do that?'

'I'll give it a go,' she said, and put her feet on the pedals.

He said, 'The pedals connect to a nose wheel to steer the plane, or the tail fin when we are airborne to keep the plane flying straight and not sideways.'

She lined the plane up on the runway.

Riley said, 'I'm standing on the brakes and increasing the revs we need a take-off speed of two hundred kilometres an hour, but we need about eight hundred metres of runway to get to that speed. They're marked off every hundred metres on the runway in white paint. You count them off and at the seven hundred mark, we should be in the air, wheels up.'

He pulled back on the yoke, and they were. They banked to the north, and the islands came into view in the distance. He adjusted the flaps and sat back. She said she would never forget the experience and thanked him.

Whoop, whoop. A horn sounded in the cockpit. The red fuel pump and oil-pressure lights flashed on the instrument panel. They were going down.

'Mayday, mayday,' Riley called over the radio and gave their position. He had not lowered the wheels in case they flipped the aircraft when they hit the water. The aircraft skimmed along the surface and came to rest in a floating position.

'Everyone, out on the wing,' he told them, as he went back and opened the side door. They went out one by one and were now standing on the wing, ankle deep in water.

The bloke from Canberra saw it first.

'Crocodiles! Crocodiles!'

Sure enough, there were little beady eyes just visible on the surface. Riley helped them all climb on the top of the fuselage. The bloke from Canberra slipped back down on the wing, which was now submerged knee-deep.

'They are saltwater crocodiles,' Riley said, 'and can crunch your bone to pieces. Quick, give me your hand.'

As he was pulling him up, the croc slid in. Snap, snap. A piece of the wing was gone and what was left of the bloke's foot was hanging on a thin shred of sinew from the bottom of his leg. Riley used his 9mm pistol to shoot the croc. Although the bullets penetrated the thick skin, they didn't seem to do much damage, and the croc came rushing back high in the air, jaws open. Riley shot it in the eyeball. It rolled over and disappeared under the wing. There were now four crocodiles circling the aircraft. They looked like they knew the plane was slowly sinking, and it was just a matter of time before they ate.

The operators at Port Melville ran a barge service for freight and the mayday call came over the air in the barge radio room. The radio operator rang the captain with the mayday details. The captain was a retired navy man and had no time for the police who had just fined him for speeding.

He said, 'Well, that's a bit of bad luck for them, isn't it? They can all sink as far as I'm concerned. Tell them we'll come and get them if they cancel my $400 speeding fine. Otherwise, tell them they're out of luck.'

But he thought about it for a while and said, 'Bugger the cop pilot, but there are other innocent people on board.'

When he received the information that the passengers were politicians, he said, 'We should let them all bloody sink! If the crocs find out who they all are, they won't have anything to do with them either. But I suppose we'd better go and get them.'

The mayday call had also been received by the police air wing and they were dispatching a helicopter to the crash site.

Riley said, 'None of this will matter if someone doesn't get here in the next fifteen minutes, because we'll all be gone.'

The police chopper was first to arrive. It had seen the barge on its way to the crash site. It had also seen the crocodiles circling. It came in low, hovering and firing bursts of rounds to keep them away from the plane, which was now just barely afloat. The barge arrived and threw chunks of meat and scraps overboard to keep the crocodiles away from the plane while they loaded the survivors onto the barge.

The captain of the barge said to Riley, 'You owe me a $400 speeding fine.'

Riley said, 'I'll see what I can do, and thanks.'

The captain said, 'Ask that bloke that lost his foot if he wants to sell his slippers.'

'Not funny,' said Riley.

CHAPTER TWENTY-SIX

Nobody seemed to know who it was that kept resupplying wood at the drovers hut, but Zach certainly appreciated it as he went out for some more from the stack. In a pitch black canvas sky, the stars were a promise of better things to come, a fresh gift for an impending new dawn. Zach looked up and he knew they were whispering him a message his ears couldn't hear. Nighttime in the outback was like opening the window of the real universe.

Dusty came out and looked up.

'A young boy called Riley once told me the night sky was calling him to fly, and that's where he is––.'

'––Did you see something moving out there?' said Zach, 'Over there near the vehicles?'

'No, it's your imagination.'

'Well, maybe...' and they went back inside with the wood.

When they came out the next morning, most of their food supplies had gone and every tyre on the vehicles had been punctured.

'Well, you did see something last night, didn't you?' said Dusty, 'And you know who it was that would have done this. There is a single tyre track leading away from the vehicles, suggesting a motorcycle.'

They did their morning radio checks and requested mechanical back-up and a resupply of stores. An hour later, one chopper arrived with a mechanic and tyre equipment and the second with stores and food resupply. Maxine had come along for the ride.

She said, 'The police will be here shortly. You're to wait and give statements.'

'We didn't see anything except those motorcycle wheel tracks over there, but, okay, we will wait for the police,' they said.

Zach wondered why the boss lady would bother to be there, as there was nothing for her to do. What he didn't know was that she knew a police helicopter was coming out, and she was secretly hoping it would be Riley.

When the police arrived, she learnt that Riley had indeed been posted to Alice Springs but had been sent on detachment to Darwin. *Just another disappointment*, she thought. *You're an idiot.* She wasn't able to answer why she was waiting all her life for something that might not eventuate. She just knew if he didn't come back, it would put a knife in her heart and she would be sad forever.

Her sister had told her on many occasions, 'Go and find him. Tell him how you feel.' But Clara often said the problem was that Maxine was still the placid, freckled face kid who was not the pushy kind, who waited for things to happen naturally, as she had watched happen with life and death on the station. That was obviously the way this would be with her love and unexplainable passion for Riley.

CHAPTER TWENTY-SEVEN

Clara was in her early thirties now and expecting their second child. Ben was a specialist paediatric doctor with his rooms at the Mater General Hospital in South Brisbane. Ben's father, Bazza, who was now a Senior Sergeant in the Water Police, had been sent on detachment with a crew and two motor vessels to Darwin. He was the skipper of one of the largest police boats, or cutters, one hundred metres in size, designed for extended operations with advanced surveillance and boarding capabilities. They would cover the nearly eighteen hundred kilometres of water that surrounds Darwin and the small coastal inlets, providing police security maritime support to the navy for the containment and movement of asylum seekers arriving by boat from Afghanistan, Iran, Iraq and Pakistan who, when they were intercepted, would be held at Manus Island.

Bazza explained over dinner with Clara and Ben, who were there visiting him, that Manus Island during the Second World War had been occupied by the Japanese in 1942. It became a US naval base, then an Australian naval base prior to New Guinea's independence.

He told them about Riley's plane going down with mechanical failure the day before on the way to the Tiwi Islands with politicians on board. They all survived, but one of the pollies lost his foot to a crocodile.

'If Riley's got nine lives, I reckon he's only got five left to play with. Does Maxine get told all this stuff about Riley?'

'No, she doesn't,' Clara said, 'We're not getting involved one way or the other. He will tell her if he wishes to, though I don't think he communicates with her at all. I spoke to him a long time ago. He said in those days it was the age barrier. Someone ten loving someone twenty wasn't going to happen, regardless of how they felt. But as years have gone by, I've told him once, someone thirty loving someone twenty is a different story. And that, my dear father in-law, is what Riley needs to be reminded of. If you see him again, and you will because he is in Darwin as well, you might over a beer give him a lesson in love that's been patiently waiting ... or maybe gone forever.'

CHAPTER TWENTY-EIGHT

Abed and Zarac had been promised a new life in Australia with guaranteed citizenship by the Islamic fundamentalist group, the Taliban, if they carried certain packages and joined the illegal boat immigrants bound for Darwin. When they arrived, they were to deliver them at a spot where they would be told along the coastline.

They were now on a wooden hundred-year-old fishing punt with eighty other illegal immigrants. The packages were in a small steel container they each carried. They had no knowledge that inside each containers was a small glass jar with ten black and orange European Paralytic beetles. Abed had the jar with the ten male beetles, and Zarac had the jar with the ten females. These beetles were also known as groin crawlers, because they worked their way up into the soft part of the groin, burrowed in and poison and paralysed the body parts within minutes. When the beetles mated, they could multiply themselves a hundredfold in one day. They could keep multiplying thousands of times in the outback cattle stations, decimating the Australian cattle and beef industry.

The plan was simple. They each had a bag of party balloons, and if it looked like they were going to be intercepted by the police or navy, they were to blow up the balloons, tie them on the containers and throw them over. Otherwise, they were to drop them off close to the shore as planned. The Taliban lookouts that were in Darwin would retrieve the packages, and it wasn't Abed or Zarac's concern what happened after that. They were to seek and find a man called Zach who worked in the mines in Tennant Creek, who would assist them to fit in with their new life in Australia.

*   *   *

Maxine had once again learnt how life can hurt. Riley was not flying the police chopper that had arrived at the drovers hut. The Double Diamond pilot felt sorry for her. She had the look of a person drained of all hope, so he gave her the controls for a small puddle jump fly back to Double Diamond.

As she lay in bed that night, she realised that almost half of Riley's life had gone; he would be now forty. Her passion had finally outgrown her patience. Yes, she would write to him, just once, and after that, she would have to be content to know her life's soul had been lost. But, yes, she would write. She decided to first consult her diary.

Dear Diary, she wrote, *how can I write to him to bare my soul and share the contents of my heart, a heart that's full of love, a heart that aches with pain and passion and longs for his sound and his scent? Oh, how I wish he were here now, a small child's flickering love flame and memories of long ago that now burns deep inside me and tugs at my inner soul. Tell me, my Private Diary, how to love and not scare away this silent lover of mine in the hope he comes back someday. Or will all this just continue until I'm old and grey and will I die of a broken heart? Will I die of a broken heart? There appears no other way. Please stay safe and come back to me, Riley.*

As her teardrops fell on the page, she slowly closed the diary and fell asleep.

The Sandman had been and her diary lay across her chest, and in her dream she walked hand in hand through the white paper daisies with Riley. They walked and talked together, smiling and laughing and when she woke in the morning, he was gone. Oh Riley, she said, you are the keeper of my soul, and the owner of my heart, please come back to me.

*   *   *

Zach and Dusty's vehicles were ready to go, the choppers had gone, they had replenished their stores and spares, said their goodbyes and headed off. The main role now for them were fences, dams, creeks and stray or sick cattle. There was always something that needed to be fixed, or out of the ordinary that needed to be reported or investigated.

The outback can play on your mind when you're on your own within its environment. In the hot dry climate, the horizon develops a shimmering haze with shapes and silhouettes, testing the brain's imagination as to what it thinks it is seeing, if anything.

Zach needed another look. He climbed on the roof of the vehicle and used the binoculars. Yes, there it was again, but what was it? Yes, it was one of those UAV things. He knew they had been testing the unmanned aerial vehicles with search and rescue competitions in previous years but these had been discontinued. Double Diamond was not yet using what they were now calling drones for mustering, so who was operating this and from where, and what was it doing? He watched it getting closer until it was high above his head. Quite a scary sensation, as if the thing were alive and was watching him.

And that's exactly what it was doing. Someone was watching.

CHAPTER TWENTY-NINE

Under the cover of darkness, the old boat managed to get within the shallows of the mangrove swamp's shoreline by the time the police launch came into view, its searchlights probing the dark for the handful of illegal immigrants who had gone overboard. Abed and Zarac left the packages in the mangroves and activated their glow sticks for retrieval. People were being rounded up out of the mangroves and taken to the police boat, but Abed and Zarac disappeared into the night. As the police boat pulled away, a single black clad figure moved out from the shadows and retrieved the packages.

The plan was to wait till after the festive season and holiday period that were popular in Australia in the outback with tours and camping. The release of the beetles was set for January and February, which meant that next week, five small drones with two male and two female beetles in each would be released from areas around Alice Springs and Tennant Creek into outback cattle stations where large numbers of cattle roamed vast areas, unsupervised for long periods of time. This would give the beetles time to multiply and create havoc among the cattle before being detected. The small self-destructing drones would fly in low, drop the beetles, gain altitude and then self-destruct.

* * *

Zach and Dusty were in their last week of bore runner duties, which was now basically just fence maintenance and cattle welfare checks. The wet season had already begun, so they needed to be back at the station by the end of the week, or they wouldn't get back at all.

Zach heard his radio calling him.

'Go ahead, Dusty,' Zach said.

'I've just seen … well, I don't know what I've actually seen,' Dusty said. 'One of those plastic flying things just came whizzing over low, hovered for a second, then flew up high and exploded. Strangest thing I ever saw. Frightened the Christ out of a couple of cows.'

'Might be kids playing with them. There was one here where I was yesterday. I'll swear it was looking at me, and someone was watching.'

They look like kids' toys to me,' said Dusty, 'but I'll report it.'

The little black and orange beetles the size of a ladybug dropped to the ground throughout the outback and scurried away to mate, multiply and find flesh.

The hot, wet monsoon season arrived, and Zach was getting ready for his last night by the fire before travelling back. *You could tell*, he said to himself, *that this is really going to turn to shit. Look how black it is now.* He decided to pack up before the deluge hit. He had trouble walking back to the vehicle, and he had a pain in the groin. He dropped his pants and saw what he thought was a tick. But no, it was some sort of beetle. Within minutes, he was paralysed from the waist down.

The storm was now on top of him. He lay shivering beside a fire that, in the storm, looked like a small candle in the night.

He lay motionless, staring at the Indian ink sky that was being relentlessly cracked open by a show of power and strength, lighting and thunder that howled and cracked like a thousand whips. The wind tore through small saltbushes and swept across the open ground. Small critters were sucked up into the whirlwind and sent high into the air. Large red clouds of dust, swirling, swirling, performed their final dance before the rain came to dampen their ego. The dry creek bed next to his campsite had filled with a torrent of fast-moving water and the soft, red soil bank next to where he lay was being washed away. He tried in vain to grope and claw himself away from the bank, but he couldn't reach the vehicle to hold on to it. The bank caved in, and Zach slid into the water.

Coming downstream behind him in the murky torrent were tree stumps, branches, pieces of barbed wire fences, a dead cow and a host of small marsupials like bilbies and dunnarts swimming for their lives. Being paralysed in the legs, he couldn't swim. He was buggered. He was going under ...

When a large stump bumped into him, he grabbed it and hung on for dear life. The rain pelted down like thin slivers of steel, hurting his head and bruising his face. The fast moving water had washed away the original creek banks and made new inlets and shallow streams, curves and bends that hadn't previously existed. Zach had been washed into one of these inlets along with the stump and was now pinned against the bank in the shallow water by the dead cow. When he looked down, there were dozens and dozens of the small black and orange beetles that had been washed in, floating all around him in the water.

'Oh, shit!' he called out, and started thrashing his arms around.

He suddenly realised the beetles were dead. They had all drowned in the flood water. And to add insult to injury, a bilby was sitting on top of the dead cow, staring at him.

CHAPTER THIRTY

Dusty had given up trying to contact Zach. He assumed he would be on his way back, or else he would have heard. He made one final sweep of the last cattle herd he came across. As he got closer, something wasn't right. Three cows and one bull were down with their back legs paralysed. He called it in to get approval to put them down.

'Don't do that,' Matilda said. 'I am on my way with Maxine. As the vet, she will know what we need to do. You just come on in while you can out of the storm.'

The short wave radio system around the cattle stations erupted with stories of cattle going down, paralysed in the back legs and having to be put down.

Maxine said, 'Matilda, this is bigger than just Double Diamond!'

They flew out in the two Robinson choppers and examined the livestock that were paralysed.

'Look at this,' Maxine said. 'That small beetle crawling away from the cow's leg and that one buried in like a tick, what the hell are they?'

Then they saw them, hundreds of them, black and orange beetles slightly larger than a ladybug, dead in the pools of ground water.

Matilda said, 'How long will the paralysis last, do we know?'

'No, we don't,' said Maxine, 'or even if it is eventually fatal.'

During the next three days, there were over two hundred cattle affected throughout the outback stations in the Northern Territory. Health authorities, government officials and entomologists from the major universities, along with police, local veterinary surgeons and cattle station owners were brought together at Charles Darwin University to find the answers from Professor Gaw, the coleopterist (an entomologist who study beetles) at the university.

'Good morning, ladies and Gentlemen,' he said. 'There are an estimated three hundred and sixty thousand species of beetles in Australia, with many more to be yet identified throughout the universe. I should warn you that identification of new species takes time. These dead beetles,' and he held them up in a jar, 'have only been in our possession for two days of research so far. However, we have had some luck where these are concerned. From previous studies, we had two of them pinned on a bug chart in a glass case. They are called the paralytic beetle, or in slang, groin crawlers. They are not an Australian beetle, and they have been introduced here just recently. The bad news is the paralysis is permanent, and they multiply at a rapid speed. But the good news is the beetles can't survive for long in wet monsoon climates, which is why you see them dying quickly in our wet season. So, given this looks like a terrorist act, they, whoever they are, had no understanding of the Australian outback. However, had they been planted in June or July, this issue would have been somewhat greater. The remedial action now is to herd cattle into large areas and burn the grass around the perimeter. The speed in which the beetles are dying in the wet should see this problem over within the week. If the police and authorities speak to me later, I can give them an idea of where the beetles originated from and the nationalities of couriers, so they can start looking for those who are responsible and still here, watching for the outcome.'

With all that had happened and the remedial action the outback stations had been required to take, it was only now that Matilda spoke to Dusty about the trip away.

'Go find Zach,' he said. 'Tell him we will meet after lunch to catch up on the trip away and any follow-up activities that might be required.'

'Well, I hate to have to tell you this,' Dusty said. 'He hasn't come back yet.'

'What? He was due back three days ago.'

'We have tried to call him, but there's no response, and vehicle travel now in the wet season to where he was is out of the question.'

'Bugger! The bloody beetle issue has taken away our normal priority response actions on someone missing. I'll talk to Maxine, tell the pilots to refuel the Robbies and we'll alert the police rescue crews.'

CHAPTER THIRTY-ONE

Abed and Zarac had been keeping a low profile in a "bottom of the barrel" backpacker boarding house on the outskirts of Darwin, along with other not-so-honest inhabitants. They had taken up labouring jobs with a bricklayer who paid cash at the end of each day. Most places in the outback, it seemed, paid cash on a daily basis and only wanted a first name. They had each saved $200 for the bus fare for the nine-hundred-and-eighty-eight-kilometre ten-hour trip to Tennant Creek and enough money to survive for another week once they got there. They were hoping they might even get a job there in the gold mine with Zach.

The illegal immigrants had now been interrogated by border force authorities, immigration, health officials and a bunch of do-gooders who managed to get involved. The information gained told them there were still two men missing, but they had no identifying information to pass on to the local and surrounding authorities, apart from their nationalities, that might give them some hope of finding them.

Abed and Zarac sat quietly on the bus as it travelled through Adelaide River, Hayes Creek and Emerald Springs. When the bus arrived at Daly Waters, the driver said the police would be waiting at Tennant Creek to search the bus for illegal immigrants.

He jokingly said over the intercom, 'So, if you are one of them, you better get off before then.'

Everyone laughed. The driver said after they had visited the Daly River, which he said was close to the town, they would be stopping for one hour at Banka Banka Station, and then on to Tennant Creek one hour further on.

Abed whispered to Zarac, 'That's when we'll be getting off.'

The bus pulled up in a designated park near the bank of the river. People got off the bus to stretch their legs. They were advised to stay away from the riverbank, as there were crocodiles in the Daly River. Two small children, a boy and a girl about nine or ten years old, were hitting a ball with a plastic racquet.

'Don't go near the river,' their mother called out.

But the ball went into the river and was floating just near the bank.

'Don't go near the ball!' Abed called out.

Too late. The girl was reaching down for the ball when the crocodile leapt out and grabbed her cardigan sleeve. Abed jumped in, tore the sleeve away from the croc and threw the girl on to the bank. The crocodile grabbed Abed in his jaws, rolled over and took him under. In a second, they were gone.

The crowd from the bus were gobsmacked at what they had just seen. Zarac just stood there, frozen. Then he saw that the driver was calling the police, and even with the unfortunate incident that had just happened with his friend, it was time to go. When the police arrived to do their interviews and write their report, Zarac was long gone.

Back on the bus, the talk was that maybe the hero and his mate were indeed the illegal immigrants the police were looking for, and they secretly hoped that this one would get away.

The Highway Patrol set up their roadblock checkpoint on the outskirts of Tennant Creek. They went through the bus, checking every passenger, and after speaking to the driver, they allowed the bus entry into town. When they arrived, the driver opened the bottom cargo hold doors and began pulling out the cases and bags while the passengers stood around waiting and watching for theirs. Suddenly from behind the cases, Zarac appeared.

'Jesus Christ!' said the driver.

The passengers started laughing. 'Don't you dare dob this bloke in,' they said to the driver. 'Look what his mate did. He saved this little girl standing here.'

'Yes, that's right,' said the girl's parents. 'Please give him the chance his mate has earned for him.'

The driver thought for a minute and said, 'Get out and get going.'

Nobody saw anything.

Zarac found a cheap backpacker hostel. Staying there were several casual workers at the mine who took him under their wing the next day and introduced him to the foreman, who went by the name of Lumpy. Zarac was learning quickly that few backpackers and casual workers used their real names in the outback, and that would suit him just fine.

Lumpy took him to the office to get information for Zarac's payslip.

The office administrator asked, 'What's your name, and try and come up with something original.'

Zarac said, 'My name is Warren, but I go by the name of Wozza.'

'That's not too bad,' she said, 'Okay, Warren, Wozza it is.'

Wozza said, 'Do you have someone working here by the name of Zach?'

'He worked here a while back,' Lumpy said, 'but he went walkabout. He's probably working on one of the outback cattle stations, I reckon.'

Wozza said, 'I was supposed to meet him here.'

'Good luck with that, mate!' Lumpy said. 'If you're going out there into Never Never Land, you will need some wheels. I have an old 1960 Ford Prefect that I could sell you cheap, if you like.'

They agreed on a price. Wozza said he would work at the mine for one week, pay for the car and head off to find Zach.

CHAPTER THIRTY-TWO

The police and the station's helicopters had located Zach's vehicle beside the fast flowing creek bed, but they failed to find him. However, he had been found days ago by an Aboriginal tribe on walkabout, hunting for food. They had taken him back to their camp and he was being cared for in one of their temporary shelters, a *mia mia*.

The police aircraft landed on the damp, usually dusty, runway at the Double Diamond station and was met by Maxine in the old roofless Suzuki, who said, 'Come on down to the homestead and I'll tell you what we know.'

When she told them Zach's name, the detective said, 'Well, that's a coincidence, isn't it? This fellow was working at the gold mine in Tennant Creek when a gold robbery occurred. It was later determined it was probably just a false count. However, let's go check his belongings.'

In Zach's quarters, the detective continued. 'Zach promised the police station the next one of the windmills he made, and this certainly looks like it to me. I will make sure he gets the $100 I promised him. It's very heavy, isn't it? A very heavy base to stop it blowing over when it's spinning, I suppose. Finding something as good as this workmanship in a place like Tennant Creek is like finding gold.'

They took the windmill and the small amount of Zach's belongings.

'I know he has an old Land Rover, but if you don't mind it staying here till this all sorts itself out, that would be good.'

Maxine said, 'That will not be a problem.'

She drove them back to the aircraft and in a cloud of red damp dust, they were wheels up and gone.

'Matilda, I wonder if this Zach bloke stole the gold. Did you know about the gold that was missing?'

'No, it wasn't something that ever came over the grapevine outback radio talk sessions that regularly occur, and I doubt anyone here would know. He seemed like a nice enough bloke, though, and very talented with his hands. Let's hope they find him.'

*   *   *

Clara and Ben had kept the test results to themselves for fear of something going wrong in the early stages of Clara's pregnancy, but at twenty weeks, they decided to let the cat out of the bag, or the baby out of the womb, so to speak. Ben had told his parents, who were over the moon with the news. Bazza said he knew where Riley was and would give him the news.

Riley often wondered how a woman who had had no time for him in his younger years could have changed her opinion of him over the years. *But then again,* he thought, *at the end of life, everyone has to dance to their own tune. There are things you do you shouldn't do, and things you haven't you should have done, and I guess that is the case for everyone if they look back through the pages of their book of life.*

*   *   *

Bunya went looking for Maxine who was amusing herself on a front-end loader. She had been told on numerous occasions by Matilda there was no need for her to work, but she loved to be on the land, to feel she was part of it and that when she was no longer alive, that she had done her bit and not just what she'd wanted, or expected others to work to supply her comforts. That was not her way. But it would be nice if she could get the one she loved so desperately into her arms before she died …

'Clara is on the phone, ma'am,' Bunya said. 'She's been trying to ring you.'

'Thank you,' she said as she took the phone.

'Hello, darling sister, and to what do I owe the privilege of this call? … Fantastic! I was beginning to think you two hadn't learnt how to make fire. So, when are you due?'

Clara said, 'About four months, give or take a week. Will you come for the birth?'

'You bet your sweet life I will! You just try and keep me away. Do you know if it's a boy or girl?'

'Yes, but we're keeping it a secret.'

*   *   *

Zarac worked the week at the mine and paid Lumpy for the car. It had storage racks in the back that held two twenty-litre fuel containers. The car's fuel tank held twenty-eight litres, and the car could travel eleven kilometres per litre with a range of about six hundred kilometres. More than enough, Zarac reckoned, to check out the cattle stations.

He had bought himself a small one-man tent and a number of freeze-dried packets of food for the trip, and he was as ready now as he would ever be. He said his goodbyes to the losers at the backpacker's lodge, using the term "lodge" very loosely, as it was a flea and mouse infested shanty. Once on his way, he knew he was going to enjoy the open spaces and narrow the chances of being caught by those looking for him, so he would be in no hurry. He reckoned he was already around two hundred and fifty kilometres into the outback, but he had no idea where he was going, or in fact where he was. He just followed this track and that track, as they had to be going somewhere, he thought.

He was sitting on the bonnet of the small Ford ute, staring into the open spaces of red dirt and saltbushes. He had been warned that he would be travelling in the wet season, which even the locals tried to avoid. Most areas off the beaten track were muddy slush and deep ravines of water that he guessed would normally be dry and dusty creek beds. In the shimmer of the distance, he could see a figure outlined. Was it human or just some animal? Was it moving? He had seen so many of the large mouse-like things he now knew were called kangaroos, two skinny camels and a half a dozen donkeys. Yes, he said to himself, it was moving, coming towards him. He had no weapons of any kind to protect himself, which out here was considered a must. He had no idea what was in the parcels he and Abed had brought into the country, but in his circumstances, if he got caught, he could be seen as a terrorist.

Then he could hear an engine or motor of some kind, and even on the wet track, whatever it was was throwing up red gravel and mud. Zarac had never seen anything like it in all his twenty-three years of life.

'What the hell is this?'

Something large and fat on a motorcycle, but what was it? Long matted hair, fingernails so long they curled under the hands, no face to look at, just a glimpse of two small beady eyes and, the most frightening thing of all, the smell this thing gave off, the smell of death.

The motorcycle pulled up, and whatever it was waddled off to the Ford ute, took a can of fuel, poured it into the motorcycle, stared at Zarac and rode off. Zarac sat there mesmerised at what had just happened and what he had seen.

How many of those things were out here in Australia?

CHAPTER THIRTY-THREE

Back at Double Diamond, a young Aboriginal boy had arrived with the news that Zach was alive at their campsite. He was being cared for, but he couldn't walk. Maxine radioed the details to the police rescue in Alice Springs, and the station's two Robbies took off, one with the boy and the other with Maxine.

When they arrived at the camp, Zach was propped up between two logs beside a large fire. A kangaroo carcass had been skinned and skewered through a stick and was being roasted above the fire. They were met by the elders of the tribe who explained that they found him in the creek wedged between the bank and a dead cow.

'We don't know what's wrong with him. He can't walk,' they said.

'Hello, Zach,' said Maxine. 'We have been worried about you. Can you tell us what happened to you?'

'I was bitten in the groin by a small orange and black beetle, and within seconds, I was paralysed from the waist down and washed into the flooded creek. Here I am, as you can see, still paralysed.'

Professor Gaw had told them, where cattle were concerned, the paralysis was permanent. But would that be the case with humans, she wondered, so it was best to say nothing and let the future medical results pan out.

The police rescue chopper arrived. *Bugger,* she said to herself, *still no Riley. Where the hell is he is flying at this moment? I may never get to see the big lug.*

* * *

Right at that moment in Darwin, Riley was getting lectured by Bazza, as requested by Clara.

'You do know, don't you, Riley, that this lady has been waiting and pining for you all these years. If you have no feelings for this woman, you owe it to her to tell her. She needs to get on with her life, what is left of it, a life that does or doesn't include you. Both Clara and Maxine are now in their thirties, and you in your forties. Are you hearing what I'm saying, mate? Look, let me put it this way. No one expects you to run to someone you have no feelings for, but you need to do one of two things. Tell her that you have admired her all these years, but your flying career has the priority over any lasting relationship. Or bloody well go and tell her you have always loved her but needed a career of your own to financially support her rather than leaning on her family inheritance ... Well? I'm waiting for a response, Flying Officer Senior Sergeant Riley!'

'Mate, let me put it this way. I was ten when Maxine was born. I was just one of the kids of a station worker, and seen as not having much of a chance in the outside world. Maxine, along with her sisters, were from different stock, an invisible social and economical background, taboo as far as fraternisation was concerned, although the family tolerated it up to a certain age. Spencer and Aileen were super supportive of who the kids played and made friends with, but

Maxine's two older sisters were very ... well, to put it mildly, up themselves, particularly for their age. I have no idea how I would feel about Maxine these days. However, I haven't forgotten I promised to go back one day, and I will. I have never corresponded in case she got the wrong message. But I will go back one day, soon.'

*   *   *

Maxine and Matilda were back at Double Diamond when the Ford Prefect ute arrived.

'You're a long way from somewhere,' they said.

Zarac said, 'I'm just pleased to find some real people out here, other than the thing I saw covered in hair on a motorcycle.'

'The Bunyip Man,' Maxine said. 'The Bunyip is the Aboriginal's equivalent to our boogie man, fiction and myths from the past.'

Wozza said, 'Nothing fictional and mythical about it. I saw this thing and it's real.'

'Are you looking for work?' Matilda said.

'No, I'm looking for a friend. His name is Zach.'

Matilda told him what had happened to Zach, and that by now he would be in the Royal Darwin Hospital.

'You are welcome to stay and work if you wish, and you could speak to Dusty, who knew and worked with Zach. His Land Rover is still here, so he will eventually come back for it,' Maxine said. 'The Flying Doctor is due here in three weeks for the children's check-ups and I'll be going back to Alice Springs with him and then on to Darwin. You could come as far as Alice with us if you decide to go to Darwin.'

'I've just come from Darwin, but I do need to find Zach, so I'll stay here and go to Alice Springs with you. I would appreciate it if you would buy me a plane ticket to Darwin when you buy yours. You can take it out of my wages.'

'No worries.'

CHAPTER THIRTY-FOUR

On the edge of the outback was a place known as Razorback Ridge, where in the late 1800s and early 1900s, gold had been found. It was now just an area of disused mineshafts, tailings and spoil heaps. Hidden at the bottom of one of the old mine shafts was a short tunnel that went to a cave. This is where Ismail and Mustafa had established themselves some time ago.

The cave had two camp stretches, a fold-up table and chairs, a portable refrigerator, makeshift shelves cut into the walls and a 240-watt generator that ran the fridge and a radio. The air vent that went up through the roof was concealed by a short hollow stump. As far as the locals were concerned, they were just a couple of blokes with nothing to do but fossick for gold. Their trips into town were limited to once a week for supplies.

Ismail and Mustafa were part of the same terrorist group in Australia, and they had been made responsible by their superiors for the delivery of the beetles by the drones that were flown from Razorback Ridge. They were also responsible for the demise of Abed and Zarac after they had delivered their packages, but that had not gone to plan. They were now waiting on the second delivery, drugs this time, to be despatched by drones to drug buyers in and around the Northern Territory. These drugs had been poisoned so as to cause brain damage and death. They had eight more drones set by computer for the various drug mules' locations.

The priority now, though, was to eliminate the loose end – Zarac. Zach, who they had used as bait to get the couriers here, had been dealt with by the beetles, a bonus that had saved them the trouble, so he was of no concern.

They received their orders on a daily basis by satellite phone from their superiors, whoever and wherever they were. They knew that Zarac was at Double Diamond, that a plane ticket had been bought in his name to Darwin and that he would be travelling to Alice with the Flying Doctor. They knew all this because the bookings and itinerary had been done over the outback radio system, which they were permanently tuned into.

The station radio squawked, 'Double Diamond, this is Foxtrot Delta Two. Inbound your location, fifteen minutes from wheels down. Over.'

'Roger that, Foxtrot Delta. A vehicle will meet you. Your arrival is most welcome.'

Maxine watched the shimmering shape of the Pilatus PC24 approaching just above the far end of the runway. The PC24, a single engine turbo prop aircraft often described as the ultimate flying intensive care unit, was used to transfer critically ill patients from remote locations to major hospital and medical facilities. It could land on unsealed runways and carry multiple patients and medical staff. The aircraft touched down with the grace of a bird, gently rolling to a stop, leaving behind it the runway's red dust cloud that acknowledged the steel bird's arrival with its own hello and welcome.

The medical staff said they would be there for two days, if that was okay.

'You do have room for two more going back, I hope,' Maxine said.

'Absolutely,' they said, 'and we will be going to Alice Springs and not Tennant Creek.'

'Yes, that is perfect. I will be going with a young fellow named Warren, or Wozza as he is called. We have a flight booked from Alice to Darwin. My sister Clara is having a baby there.

The doctor said, 'How time flies! My predecessor bought your sister Clara into the world. Please give her our regards.'

Ismail and Mustafa had set themselves up at the end of the runway. They had laid coils of old barbed wire across the runway three-quarters along the way and were waiting in the long spinifex grass with rifles. Zarac had been invited to sit up with the pilot for the flight. On board were the doctor, one nurse, an Aboriginal woman and her three-year-old daughte. The plane leapt forward and took off down the runway, Matilda waving as the plane sped by. They were gathering speed. Forty knots, fifty knots, seventy knots ...

'Shit, what's that?' yelled the pilot, when he saw the barbed wire across the runway.

He pulled back on the yoke as hard as he could, but just when he thought they had made it, the wheels caught the coils of wire and pulled the plane violently sideways. Three small holes appeared in the windscreen, and a larger red hole in Zarac's head. The plane skewed off the runway, destroying itself on the only boab tree for miles around.

Matilda watched it all unfold and sped down the runway to the now barely recognisable aircraft. He radioed back to the station office, and they informed the police and medical services in both Alice and Tennant Creek.

The inside of the aircraft was a mess. Seats had been torn from their positions and the stretcher bed had been ripped from its mounts. The Aboriginal woman and the child were hanging upside down, still in their seatbelts, the nurse and the doctor were scattered around inside the plane, and somehow Maxine had been thrown out and was lying unconscious under what was left of a wing. Wozza was dead with a bullet to the head and the pilot also dead with a broken neck.

Within the hour, there were two fixed wing aircraft and two rescue helicopters at the scene. During the investigation, Matilda said he heard a vehicle leaving the area somewhere but was too intent on rescuing or checking the passengers on the plane to see anyone or anything. All the injured passengers were taken straight to Royal Darwin Hospital.

When Maxine woke out of her induced coma, Clara was sitting beside the bed smiling.

'I'm sorry, but you have missed him again, darling. Riley's detachment finished two days ago, and he is now back at Alice Springs.'

'It's just not meant to happen, is it?'

'The good news is, the doctors assured me you are going to make a full recovery.'

'Why the hell would someone want to kill me and the others?'

'It wasn't you they were after. It was the one called Wozza they wanted.'

'Who's they?' Maxine said.

'No one seems to know. Wozza had no identification, so they think he might have been one of the illegal immigrants they were looking for, but it's still early in the investigation. The main concern now is, who's behind all this, and how does Double Diamond fit in it all, or is the station's involvement purely coincidental.'

CHAPTER THIRTY-FIVE

smail and Mustafa were pleased with themselves at the outcome, the removal of a loose end. That was, until they advised their superiors over the radio, then all hell broke loose.

'You are nothing but uneducated cannon fodder. Fools! If I had my way,' said the voice on the radio, 'you would both be eliminated immediately. However, that is a decision for someone else. Your only responsibility was to despatch the beetles quietly and with little attention to yourselves. Do you have any idea what will happen now? Obviously not. We now have had to devise a plan to take away the authorities' attention from you at Razorback Ridge when the drugs arrive for your next delivery by drones. Your instructions now are simple. The drugs' instructions and locations will have now been delivered in five separate packages to Double Diamond cattle station. You are to collect them, and the station is to be burnt to the ground. There are to be no survivors. In each of the packages is a post office box number that will give you access to each of the drugs to be delivered by a drone. You will be given extra manpower support at the drug pick-up point. Is that clear?'

'Yes, sir,' the two of them said. 'We will not fail you.'

'If you do,' the voice said, 'the consequences for you will be unimaginable.'

* * *

A crime think tank was set up at Tennant Creek run by a superintendent and a profiler from the Russell Street Homicide division in Melbourne. Superintendent Lucas and Senior Profiler Penelope Jane were flown to the crime scene at Double Diamond to gather initial crime scene information before a meeting was held. They were met by Matilda in the old Suzuki, and Penny gave him the mailbags for the station from the plane. They were shown their accommodation. It was a busy time now after the wet season. Cattle were being rounded up and herded into stockyards for the usual health checks after their prolonged isolation during the wet season.

'Tell us about the people here,' said Penelope.

Matilda said, 'Most of them have been here all their lives; some of them were born here. We, like most outback stations, have casual workers who come and go, backpackers and the like. No one knows their background or their history. We're happy if they put a day's work in and behave themselves, and if there are no issues, we are happy to employ and pay them. Some of them come very experienced and others are just simple labourers.'

'Tell us about the recent ones, those who have been here in the last six years. Who might have stood out, and who aren't here now?'

Matilda gave a full rundown of workers past and present and a guided tour of the station, which included the barn hanger that held the two Robinson helicopters and the two-seater 150 Cessna fixed wing aircraft. He explained that the homestead was still the owner's home and was out of bounds. Penny said there was no need to go there and later, if there was, they needed the owner's permission or a warrant.

*   *   *

'Good morning to you all,' said the superintendent at the Tennant Creek police station. 'You have been selected to be here because you may have had something to do with the latest crimes at the Double Diamond station, or you will be assisting with the ongoing investigation. I would like to introduce to you Victoria's top profiler, Chief Inspector Penelope Jane.'

She said, 'Sit back, ladies and gentlemen and fasten your seatbelt. It will be a long session. On the whiteboard, I have listed the information that we have so far, and what I make of it when it's all put together. For the benefit of the visitors, the Double Diamond station runs three thousand head of cattle, mostly Brahmans on three thousand square kilometres of outback land bordered by boundary fences and bores. They are situated three hundred and eighty kilometres from where you sit in here in Tennant Creek. The people who work these stations are tough like the land they work in, and for the most part are strong in moral fibre. It's not unusual for them to die on the very station they were born on, such is their loyalty to the land and the job they do. However, there are casual travellers like backpackers and nomads who travel from job to job, and it's those types who work at Double Diamond that I am going to focus on. They are listed on the whiteboard as players one to four. Player one was the first contract manager who was, according to the owner, not a suitable person for the job. He was argumentative and was asked to leave. He left the station on his motorcycle and has never been seen or heard of since. He was eventually replaced by the contract company. Player two was the workshop foreman. His name was Steven Slowgo, also known as Bolta. He stole a Land Cruiser and convinced the eldest Roper daughter called Jessy to go for a ride with him. They found the vehicle submerged and the girl's body in the flooded creek. He is wanted for her murder. He also has never been seen again. Player three, a man called Zach who worked at the goldmine during the mysterious disappearance of two gold bars, is a talented tradesman who makes model windmills. He worked at the station as a bore runner. He was bitten by beetles and is currently in Royal Darwin Hospital, paralysed from the waist down. Player 4, someone calling themselves Warren or Wozza, looked Middle Eastern and worked for a short time at the gold mine and then at the station. He was shot in the head in a plane as it sped down the runway at the station.'

Penny went on. 'Listed also on the whiteboard are other activities that may fit into this crime scene. Small black and orange paralytic beetles were released by drone to kill beef cattle in the Australian outback at about the same time a boatload of illegal immigrants was captured on the Darwin coast, thanks to Bazza from the Water Police who is here today. Two immigrants escaped, and we think this Wozza was one of them. We also know that Middle Eastern terrorists have a permanent nest of operatives here in Australia who lie dormant until called to support an act of terror, and we think that there will be more to come. We think the recent killing and plane crash was a clean-up of loose ends from the delivery and release of the beetles. All this at the moment is just speculation, but solid speculation. Feel free to take notes from the board or talk to me later if you wish. Thank you for your attendance and your attention today.'

CHAPTER THIRTY-SIX

Maxine arrived back at the station while the investigation was in progress and was told she would ber further questioned if it was considered necessary.

Maxine and Matilda were discussing what to do with the mystery packages that were in the mailbags they had just opened. They were addressed to the station with the following instructions on the wrapping: "Please do not open. These packages are travelling safe hand and will be picked up personally within one week of delivery."

'Considering what's going on at the moment,' Maxine said, 'these packages are a ticking time bomb. Not that I'm expecting them to explode, but obviously someone's coming for them, and I'm suspecting the outcome won't be nice. We need to let the investigation team know about them, but not over the radio, just in case the wrong ears out there are listening. Mind you, I could be exaggerating this whole cloak-and-dagger stuff, but I doubt it with what's been happening. Why it's all happening here, who would know?'

Riley, being stationed at Alice Springs, was fully aware of all the details of the latest plane crash, the investigation and who was involved. His mate, Bazza, had been keeping him up to date on a daily basis. And although Bazza was Water Police and out of his depth (if you pardon the pun), he was involved due to the illegal imigrants' suspected involvement.

Riley had had enough of the secondhand rumours and innuendos from those of his workplace. It was time he found out for himself, so he took long service leave. He headed back into his memories where he knew there would be a bundle of mixed feelings that would bubble to the surface. He would have to decide how he would face some personal truths, but they needed to be faced head on.

And then there was Maxine, an entirely new Pandora's box. Who knew what that would bring? Was this the wrong time, given the investigation was still on going? No more bloody excuses! He hadn't seen her for years. What did she look like now? Maybe she had a glass eye or no nose; was her brain all right after the plane crash? Jesus, she might hate him and shoot him on sight for taking so long to come back! How long was it? Almost thirty years!

*   *   *

He drove in through the stone entrance that he had fallen off so many times as a small boy. A woman came out of the main homestead dressed in a blue and white checked top and a long white apron. Yes, it was her. There was no mistaking the freckles and the Shirley Temple hairstyle. A slight smear of red lipstick now seemed to bring her face alive. She was slender and carried herself with an air of grace and importance. She had developed into a beautiful woman.

She was running now, calling out, 'Is that you, Riley?' She ran up to within a foot of him and looked up into his eyes. Hers were full of tears.

'You came back!' she said. 'I knew you would. I have waited

so long for this moment. We have so much to talk about, so much to share. You look so good, Riley,' and she threw her arms around him.

He looked closely at her and he could see that in amongst this harsh, barren land with its red dust and barbed wire, this little girl he remembered had become a woman. She had immediately made quite an impact on him. She wasn't beautiful in terms of a perfect figure, but her skin was flawless and the few freckles she had retained from her childhood days only seemed to enhance her beauty. In her younger days he remembered she could produce a smile by curling up the left corner of her mouth, like a fox who had just spotted an unguarded hen house. But at this moment, the twitch of her lips gave a glimmer of delight and a hint of mirth, yes, he said to himself, she was a beautiful woman. But was he to late. But then again, nothing's to late if you love it.

He took his bedroll from the vehicle.

'What are you doing?'

'I'll be camping down with the workers.'

'Oh no, you won't,' she said, 'You're not just one of the workers. You're family, and don't you forget it, Riley. You will be staying in the family homestead along with those of us who are still here.'

He realised there was no sense in arguing about it. She had earned the right to take the lead, so he smiled and said, 'Thank you for your hospitality, and yes, we have a lot to reminisce and talk about.'

Where this was going was going to be decided very soon, he felt, but whatever the outcome, he was convinced he had done the right thing coming back. And he had to admit she was already pulling at his heart strings. That little girl had somehow managed to unknowingly crawl into his heart and lain there dormant over the years.

They sat by the large, open, stone fireplace in the central kitchen and lounge area with Bunya going back and forth with wine refills and wood for the fire, trying not to let them see the smile on her face. She had at one time said to Maxine, 'Please excuse me, ma'am, for speaking out, but you deserve the best, and the best, ma'am, is Riley. And I wish you all the Rileys in the world.' Even Bunya could see that the yearning for Riley was much more than a bush girl's hope for a city life, as Maxine was a professional woman in her own right.

* * *

Back at Razorback Ridge, as promised, Ismail and Mustafa had been joined by a red ragging support group who were prepared to die for a cause that they had no idea about. They had brought with them ten firebomb self-destructing drones, to be released from the old mine site.

The best plans were usually made simple for stupid people. Ismail drove up to the front entrance of the homestead and was meet by Riley who had been out early for a look around the station. Each time he saw things that had remained the same as he remembered them, it brought a smile to his face.

'Where did you come from?' Riley said.

'I've come from a long way to pick up my packages,' Ismail said.

Maxine came out of the homestead and told him to go down to the station office past the stockyards and ask for Matilda.

'What's all that about?' Riley asked.

Chapter Thirty-Six

She told him about the packages and the instructions.

'I don't like the smell of this at all,' Riley said. 'Something bad is going down.'

'I'm here to pick up the packages,' Ismail told Matilda.

'How do I know who you are?' Matilda said

Ismail pulled out his gun. 'Just get the packages right now.'

Matilda came out with two.

'Where are the rest?'

'That's all that there were.'

'Bullshit! There are five of them.'

'Well, we only got two.'

'I'll count to three, said Ismail, 'and you'll be dead if I don't have them.'

A voice from behind them said, 'A grown man should know his strengths and weaknesses and know where he fits in comfortably,' and Ismail was shot dead by Riley.

'I can't believe I've just seen that!' said Matilda.

'Well, I am a police officer,' Riley said, 'and he was obviously a bad dude.'

In the radio shack, electronic weather monitoring equipment was set up to detect changes in air turbulence to give them early warnings of meteorological changes. Everything about the weather centred from this radio shack. Suddenly, a loud siren came on, warning them of unexpected air turbulence approaching the station.

'That's strange,' said Riley. 'There's not a breath of breeze anywhere for a hundred kilometres, so what's setting off the sensors?'

CHAPTER THIRTY-SEVEN

/'Good morning and thank you for your attendance again today,' said Penelope Jane. the profiler. 'Yesterday, we received a message from Double Diamond that five strange packages were received and were to be picked up by safe hand by someone today. This morning, we received another radio message that a man of Islamic appearance had been shot by an off-duty police officer who was visiting the station. The man was attempting to take the packages and had the station manager held up at gun point. The last transmission was that they were under some sort of aerial attack before the transmission went dead.

'The air wing are on their way there now, and we have been allocated an aircraft to follow up the investigation at the station. The local police chief, here with us today, has reported that a minibus with a load of men of Islamic appearance arrived there yesterday and have not been seen since. Who, and where, are they? I doubt they are just tourists. We are waiting for them to be tracked down, then we will move in on whatever it is they're up to. The outlying areas of the old gold mine sites are being scanned as I speak, and all other outlying areas where unobserved activities might take place within a fifty-kilometre radius. It all just seems too much of a coincidence that these people in the bus have arrived right now with what's been happening.'

*   *   *

'What's that humming noise? It's getting louder.' Riley said.

'Look, there are drones, lots of them,' said Matilda.

'Quickly, Maxine, get everyone inside the cyclone bunkers and meet me at the helicopter barn,' said Riley. 'I will push one out, and you're coming with me with a shotgun.'

The drones were like large buzzing mosquitoes whizzing through the air, going every which way, dive bombing into buildings and exploding. Some of the station hands were trying to shoot the drones, but the drones were too fast and manoeuvrable. Riley and Maxine lifted off in the chopper and climbed up above where the drones were buzzing around the station.

Riley said, 'They are being operated remotely from somewhere near. Each one has its own operator. There must be an "eye in the sky" sending pictures to the individual operators ... Yes, there it is up there, Maxine, the drone that's twice the size of the others. See? The revolving camera swivelling around hanging underneath the drone?'

Maxine loaded the shotgun and as they flew past the camera drone, she blew it to pieces.

'Well done. Give the lady a kewpie doll,' said Riley. 'I'll do what I can to get close enough, and the rest are yours, my love.'

He was too busy flying to see her blush. All she said was, 'It's like being in a shooting gallery.'

Four of the station outbuildings, the stockman single men's quarters and the bulk fridge freezer building had been blown up. There were still three drones left that hadn't self-destructed into a building.

'We'll go down low,' Riley said, 'and get the one there that's just hovering.'

When they approached the drone, it flew straight into the helicopter's tail rotor. Round and round and down and down they went. Luckily, they weren't far off the ground. As the chopper hit the ground, they climbed out just as the last drone flew itself into the chopper, blowing it to pieces. People came running out from the cyclone bunkers with hoses and buckets of water, rescuing livestock, vehicles and machinery from burning buildings and barns. The second helicopter and the Cessna 150 fixed wing aircraft were untouched in their hanger, hidden among the hay bales. There had been a hundred and fifty cattle in the stockyards for checking and grading for sale; they were now spread out down the runway, spooked by the explosions.

Two police aircraft circled above the station, trying to land. The second Robinson chopper was now in the air, heading the cattle away from the runway as the first of the fixed wing planes came in, ploughing red dust into the air, coming to rest as the second plane rolled in behind it. The police in the aircraft were met by Maxine, Matilda and Riley with three vehicles to transport them all back to the station's dining hall area for the meeting and the investigation. It was agreed that by the time they did all the necessary forensic checks, and the coroner dealt with Ismail's body, they would need accommodation for two nights.

Penny and her group were allocated a space in one of the barns to set up their investigations, which was separate from the coroner's and the forensic team's. They were all surprised to see Riley, who they knew from their areas of the police force. No one knew his background in regards to the Double Diamond station, so they had no idea why he was there. Some of them imagined he was on an undercover assignment.

Riley had never told anyone in the force, apart from his mate Bazza, about his younger station days, particularly about the boy's body that was buried here by Bolta years ago. He was undecided what he would do regarding that. Surely, they would understand he was only a small boy and scared to death when that had happened. But now he was a mature individual, and a police officer to boot, he had a responsibility to report the incident and recover the boy's body, or what was left of it, he guessed. But for now, there seemed to be more important issues to be dealt with.

*   *   *

At the meeting in the barn, Penny said, 'I will share with you now the latest intelligence we have received from our military partners who have their own investigation running alongside ours. The drones used here are called combat or kamikaze drones, designed explode upon impact with their target. The "eye in the sky" drone was a reconnaissance drone equipped with high resolution cameras, thermal sensors and other surveillance equipment which had jammed the station's radio equipment. The drones were operated from a ground control station located nearby. These stations rely on a complex network of satellites and communication cables to transmit commands and receive data from the drones. They use GPS and other navigation systems to determine their position and follow pre-programmed flight paths determined by the operators.

'Our intelligence tells us this complex system will be underground here somewhere and would have been here for some time to have been set up with the specialist equipment.

The authorities are scanning the areas now searching for electronic disturbances and unusual high radar frequencies.'

*   *   *

A voice came over the Islamic radio from within the mine.

'If we have to come and do this ourselves, you will be breathing your last breath. I want those aircraft at Double Diamond destroyed by the kamikaze explosive drones you have left. You are to retrieve those packages for the drug pick-up locations – or else!'

CHAPTER THIRTY-EIGHT

Two large explosions erupted that sent police and authorities running out of the meeting to investigate. The station workers who were repairing or cleaning up from the earlier bombing were stopped in their tracks. Everyone headed in the direction of the plumes of fire and black smoke that was coming from the end of the runway. Both police aircraft that had been parked on the side of the runway were blown to pieces, now just a heap of twisted plastic and metal. What was left of the seats, engine parts and propellers was scattered over fifty metres. While they stood and watched, the last of the kamikaze drones zeroed in on the shack with the radio antenna and destroyed the station's communications to the outside world. Thankfully, there was nobody inside, as everyone had come out to see the aircraft explosion. Internal communication was via their own cable-run internal phones spread throughout the station, and all vehicles had two-way radios to each other and back to the station, as did the helicopters and the Cessna fixed wing aircraft. Mobile phones were useless.

Riley said to Maxine, 'Go and get the five packages and meet me in the aircraft barn. I'll have the other chopper ready to go. They will have to send the station cars back for help, but in this country, that's a five-hour trip to cover three hundred kilometres.'

With all the commotion of the explosions and everyone running in the same direction, nobody saw the two terrorists drive their Jeep round behind the homestead past the stockyards full of Brahman bulls to look for the five packages.

Riley was in the barn filling the chopper with a hand pump from a drum of avgas fuel.

'Where do you think you're going?' The terrorist pointed a gun at Riley. 'Where are the packages?'

'Don't know about any packages,' said Riley, 'and if you shoot that gun in here, you'll be blown up along with me and this drum of fuel. Now, look, Australia is the place of a fair go for everyone, so how about it?'

'What does that mean?' the terrorist said.

'It means he doesn't like you, you idiot,' Maxine said, who had come up behind him.

She rammed the long five-pronged hay fork through his neck, pinning him to a wooden roof support pole.

She went up close to him, looked him in the eye and said, 'You wouldn't know a fair go if it spat in your face,' and that's exactly what she did.

As they threw the packages in the chopper and pushed it out of the barn, Matilda released fifty Brahman bulls from the stockyards. As they came bellowing between the buildings, the second terrorist was forced into his Jeep. He could see the people with the chopper had the packages but there was nothing he could do. He decided it was a lost cause and drove off. Down the road he pulled over and watched the chopper take off with the packages on board. He knew that was not going to be a good outcome for him on his return to the mine.

They lifted off and banked away over the homestead. Maxine was scared witless; she couldn't believe this was all happening. It was like watching a movie, the fair maiden and her hero lover who had returned, and together in a final shootout, they would save the day.

'Stop daydreaming,' Riley said, 'Find out what's in those packages, and fill that extra magazine for the rifle with bullets. Tennant Creek by road is three hundred and ten kilometres. The way we'll fly is two hundred and thirty-five kilometres. Staying on normal cruise, we have a range of around four hundred kilometres. We will follow that Jeep to its destination then double-back to one of the drum top-up points, fill up and radio their location to the police. So, what's in the packages?'

Maxine said, 'There is a post office box number and a key in each package for the post office at Daly Waters.'

'That's interesting, isn't it? I think, once we report the terrorist location, the goodies will be very busy chasing the baddies. So, I think we should follow the packages. After all, I am a police officer, aren't I, my dearest?'

"My dearest." Was she game to imagine how much he meant by that? She hadn't spent enough time with him to pinpoint how he expressed himself. She remembered from their young days how sometimes he was hard to read. She decided she would need to be very careful after all these years of waiting for her prince. She might not have grown her hair long enough to be rescued from her tower.

'There's the Jeep down there, crossing that gully,' Maxine said.

'We'll bank away now and tuck in above and behind him,' Riley said.

They followed the Jeep as it drove into the old gold mining area. They watched it driven down a dug-in slope and disappear.

'Well, that's it,' Riley said. 'We know where they all are.'

CHAPTER THIRTY-NINE

Because the chopper radio was linked to the station vehicles, Riley was able to notify the people coming from the station by the outback tracks. He gave them the mine's location, told them what was in the packages and where Maxine and he were going.

'Daly Waters is right on our flying range limit,' Riley said, 'so we will need to drop into Elliott for fuel. There's a fuel station and roadhouse there where we can refuel from their drums of avgas. Elliott is about two hundred and fifty kilometres from us here at Tennant Creek, so we can puddle jump the last hundred and fifty kilometres to Daly Waters with no problems.'

'Let's go, then,' Maxine said, 'We are burning daylight. Where do we land when we get to Daly Waters?'

'At the old airfield built in 1928. It's the site of Australia's first international airport, with Qantas and other airlines using it in the 1930s. It was used extensively for overseas mail runs and in World War Two, saw a huge amount of movement of aircraft, supplies and troops. And so, my little turtle, that's where we will be landing.'

Once again, the affectionate term didn't go unnoticed.

They landed in Elliott at the rear of the petrol station where the fuel drums were kept. Maxine got food and drinks from the roadhouse while Riley refuelled the chopper. He also made some calls about police attendance at Daly Waters police station, which was normally unattended. He was informed that someone from the narcotics branch in Melbourne called Inspector Tobias would be there for the week, investigating a tip-off about a possible large drug transfer that was rumoured to be occurring at Daly Waters.

No, Riley thought, *it can't be him! Last I heard, he was a motorbike cop in the road trauma division of the highway patrol.*

As they took off, he gave Maxine the latest information.

'A drug transfer? That's just too much of a coincidence, isn't it, Riley?'

They flew in over the top of the Daly Waters pub and banked around over the police station as a "hello, we are here message" and landed at the airfield. As Riley was securing the rotor blades down, a four-wheel drive vehicle arrived, and the bloke in a singlet and shorts got out.

'Hello there,' Maxine said. She introduced herself, and ...

'That's Flying Officer Senior Sergeant Riley,' the bloke said. 'Riley, you old bastard, what the hell are you doing here?'

'Well, bugger me!' Riley said, 'Toby, the other motorcycle kid. Where's the two-wheeler?

'I transferred years ago, mate, dead-end job. As you can see, more advancement and tourist class travelling with narcotics. Jesus, you're looking good. Who's the girlfriend?'

'Let's get to the pub, book in, get freshened up and a drink. We will explain everything and compare notes.'

* * *

The first Double Diamond vehicle to arrive at the mine site location brought profiler Penny, Bazza and the two detectives from Tennant Creek. The main support group were still an hour away. After a quick discussion, they decided not to wait for the back-up team. Guns drawn, staying close to the wall of the slope, down they went.

Further down the shaft, they could see lights and hear the low frequency, humming sound of a generator. The narrow passage opened into a large area. A man dressed in traditional *shalwar kameez* was sitting at a high tech radio transmitter. A message in Morse code was coming in, but the long and short beeps were unrecognisable, being in a foreign language.

Just inside the large area was another passage going off to the left. Penny and Bazza headed down towards the light and the voices. The Tennant Creek detectives stayed to cover their rear and the mine's entrance. There were four men in the second enclosure, also all dressed in traditional *shalwar kameez*. Each one had an electronic computer-like device connected to a strange looking aerial. Bazza whispered that they would be the drone operators responsible for the demolition at the cattle station.

'And see those two pipes going to the roof? That's how they get their air in here.'

Penny whispered, 'All this will have something to do with what's in the post boxes at Daly Waters that Riley and Maxine have gone after. Where is that minibus full of men that we are all looking for? I didn't see it parked here anywhere, and there's not enough of them here. Whoever they are, they are waiting for something to happen or for further instructions. My gut tells me they are all at Daly Waters, and if they are, that won't be good for Riley and Maxine.'

They could hear the back-up troops coming into the mine behind them with the detectives.

Bazza said, 'We need to go back and tell them there's no need to come in any further. They need to find the two air pipes coming out of the mine shaft, remove the cowling tops and drop down a grenade.'

But before they could move to share this information, a goon came out from a narrow tunnel and said to the radio man, 'Have we received the diamond payment arrangements yet for the drugs from our African friends?'

'Yes.'

CHAPTER FORTY

The Daly Waters pub was a magnet for interstate and overseas travellers, so to sort out who was involved in transporting the drugs was nearly impossible, unless of course they were of Middle Eastern appearance. They would warrant a second look, apart from everyone else there who had a four-wheel drive and camping equipment.

The previous night, Riley and Maxine had given Toby a history lesson on the past proceedings. This morning, they were on their way to the Daly River Post Office. They showed the lady there the list of post office box numbers and the keys.

She said, 'We don't have any boxes by those numbers. There are only fifty-five people who live here, and our mailboxes only go to fifty. Your number boxes are seventy-five to eighty, so I'm afraid I can't help you.'

That night at the pub, they talked to the owner about the post boxes.

'You're looking in the wrong place.'

'What do you mean?'

'See how that's been written as AMF PO Box 75? That is an Australian Military Forces post office box, at the old airfield. That's where you should be looking.'

'Well, I'll be buggered,' they all said. 'Do us a favour – you know nothing of any of this, or where we are going tomorrow.'

'Absolutely,' he said, 'Mum's the word.'

The next morning, they headed off to the old airfield. Riley asked Toby what weapons he had in the vehicle. He said he had a stun grenade, a Berreta pump action single barrel five shot shotgun, a 7.62 mm self-loading rifle with 25-round magazines, and his 9mm pistol. He also said that the Daly River Police Station had an armoury which he knew the code for entry if they needed anything else.

'Good,' said Riley. 'We need to go via the chopper to pick up our Browning over and under shotgun.'

The two men would have a shotgun each, the rifle would stay in the vehicle and Maxine would have Toby's 9 mm pistol.

Because the old airfield was a tourist attraction, cars were occasionally coming and going around the airfield buildings, so the two hired Land Cruisers went unnoticed, parked between the old administration building and an old corrugated iron hut that at one time had been the Officers Club. A sign above the administration building said, "Military Post Office and Paymasters Office. 0900hrs–1600hrs. Uniforms must be worn at all times on pay parades." They drove around the airfield to get a feel for the general layout.

'There's the post office over there, next to that old shed that looks like an igloo,' said Maxine.'

'That's called a Nissen hut,' said Toby.

'Well, whatever it is, it's next to where the post office boxes will be. With these tourists coming and going, it's not an ideal situation, given what we have to do.'

Riley said, 'I'll guarantee we aren't the only ones here for what's in the boxes, and Toby didn't come all this way just to see me, so that should tell you something.'

'Do we have a plan, or do we just fudge it?' said Maxine.

'My suggestion would be,' said Riley, 'that each of us take a key and bring whatever is in that box back to the car. That would be at least three boxes in our possession if, for some reason, we can't get back for the last two. I'm probably making a mountain out of a mole hill, but I know you all know the seven p's: prior preparation and planning prevents piss poor performance. If anyone has a better idea, let's hear it; otherwise, we're good to go.'

They parked the car off to the side of the building, took a key and box number each and went into the veranda opening to the mailboxes. Inside each mailbox was a package of drugs attached to a small drone. They each grabbed a drone and turned to head for the vehicle.

There were four terrorists in each Land Cruiser. They saw the action had started.

'Go, go, go!' one of them screamed.

'They are blocking us in,' Maxine called out. 'Get this one with the beard!'

'Maxine, they've all got a bloody beard!'

'I mean the one that's coming for me with a knife!'

A shotgun blast echoed through the veranda. The terrorist with the knife was now staggering around without a head.

Toby called out, 'I'll give you covering fire. You make a break for the vehicles and use the stun grenade I gave you, Maxine, on your way past. Riley and I will do the rest.'

The terrorists were firing automatic weapons as they took cover behind some old wooden lunch tables. Toby and Riley pumped two shotgun rounds into one of the terrorists' vehicles. They kept their heads down, allowing Maxine to run to the police vehicle. On the way past, she dumped the stun grenade into the Land Cruiser. The stun grenade shattered the windows, and three bearded blokes staggered out, noses bleeding and ears ringing. Toby and Riley appeared and cut them in half with the shotguns.

'Let's go, let's go!'

With Toby behind the wheel, Riley climbed in and pulled Maxine in on the move. The remaining Land Cruiser had come out from behind the administration building and was coming after them.

'Well, that was exciting, wasn't it?' Maxine said.

'Yes but it's not over yet, my love,' Riley said.

There it was again – those tender words. A reaction, not for her benefit at all?

The two vehicles speed off down what had been the main runway of the old airfield. A tourist vehicle coming out of the scrub onto the runway had to swerve sideways. It flipped over twice and went back into the bush. Holes were appearing in the rear of the unmarked police car from the automatic gunfire from behind. Maxine broke the back window out and returned fire with the long-range rifle with the thermal infrared scope.

They were very close now and Maxine could clearly see the front passenger who was doing the firing. She aimed the rifle and when she saw the red dot appear on his forehead, she squeezed the trigger. The small red dot became a large red hole and the firing stopped.

'It's very hard to lose these bastards in the open spaces like this, but we need to and get back to the post office boxes for the last two drone packages,' said Toby.

'Okay, Riley said. 'Get as far in front of them as you can, then get around behind the Nissen hut. Stay over near the long spinifex grass and I'll jump out. If they don't see me, and you keep going, they should follow you. I'll get the last two packages and head for the chopper while you're leading them away from me.'

They took the side road that was once the taxiway to the apron and hanger. This gave them some time as it caught the enemy off guard. They shot round behind the old buildings and Riley jumped out with the shotgun and post office keys. He rolled into the long grass and watched the Land Cruiser speed past.

There were quite a few tourists around the front of the building, so Riley shoved the shotgun down the leg of his pants and walked around to veranda. He stopped when he heard a woman tell her husband to stand still for a photo. As he touched one of the mail boxes, he was shot. The woman screamed, the husband dropped to the ground, and so did Riley.

Jesus, Riley said to himself, *that was going to be me!*

Riley pushed the crying woman off the veranda and dragged her husband's body out. There was no more shooting. It was obvious you only got shot if you looked like you were going to open a mailbox.

The woman screamed out, 'Call the police! Someone, call the police!'

Riley said, 'I am the police. I am sorry about your husband. Please be quiet. If you keep screaming, someone will shoot you as well.'

That did the trick: the screaming changed to a muffled sobbing. Riley's shotgun was useless as the shooter was way out of range of the shotgun. He tried his phone – just as he suspected, no service. He needed to contact the others. They couldn't keep driving around, if that's what they were still doing. He needed help, and probably so did they. He made a dash for the hanger where his little Robinson R22 helicopter was. He took the tie downs off the main rotor blades, did a really rough preflight check and lifted off. Once he got airborne, he started trying different police channels. Bingo! Over the radio came Maxine's voice.

'We are trapped in an old air raid bunker at the end of the main runway and taking fire.'

'Can they get to you?'

'No, but we'll be out of ammo soon.'

'Ask Toby for the code to the police station armoury.'

'It's Whisky November 1739 Alpha,' she said, 'same as the front door.'

'Roger that, Riley said. 'Hang in there. Help is on the way.'

He flew above the Daly River Road to the police station, banked away and went in over the top of the barbed wire fences with the rotor blades sucking the red dust from the road, covering the fences in a dusty orange tinge.

The building didn't look like a police station but there was a small metal blue sign under a tree that said it was. He landed the chopper on a large clearing off to one side across the road next to an old water tank on a stand.

He punched the code into the keypad at the locked front door and went in. In the back section were two small cells and next to them was a solid steel door with another keypad. Once the code was entered, the door swung open to reveal an array of weapons, most of which had been confiscated from people travelling through the area, or were old weapons handed in from surrounding farms and stations. There was, however, what he had hoped there would be, and it all went into a hessian bag: six boxes of 9 mm rounds, a box of fifty 7.62 rounds, a box of fifty shotgun shells, six grenades, two stun grenades, and two door breaching explosive packs. What the

Daly River police station would want with half this stuff he didn't know, but he would remember to thank someone. He locked up and lifted off with his goodies in the bag at his feet.

Over the chopper radio, he said, 'Stand by, my little elves. Santa is on his way with a bag of presents, so I hope you've been good.'

Maxine acknowledged the call by clicking the mike switch twice.

He climbed high and banked out over the Daly River, coming over the trees above where the Land Cruiser was hidden behind what was left of a concrete building wall. He swung in low, pulled the pin and dropped the grenade. They were standing outside the vehicle in the open and were blown to pieces by the shrapnel when the grenade exploded. They never had a chance.

Riley landed and they resupplied their ammo. They shared the grenades, two each for Toby and Maxine, and Riley kept the last one. They spent the next thirty minutes sharing information and devising the next move. Riley had sent out messages for assistance over different channels while he was in the air but had had no response. The likelihood of help coming was probably zilch. Riley told them about the sniper and the death of an innocent person. But they still needed to sit there till he refuelled from the drums he had seen, and then they would move back to the main airfield together.

Toby said, 'We will have the high ground with the "eye in the sky", and Riley can direct us to our best positional advantage point. Don't forget, our only priority is the mailboxes. Let's try not to make this like Custer's last stand.'

The radio in the vehicle squawked. 'Lifting off now,' Riley said, 'You go along the taxiway. I'll go out over the post office.'

'Roger that' came the reply.

Riley climbed high enough to get a good look at the entire airfield and its surrounds. Bad news travels fast, particularly if there's been a shooting or some sort of crime, and the spectator flies that seem to come from nowhere were gathering around the airfield. Riley guessed once the pub found out about a shootout at the "Old Okay Airfield", a mob would gather around, and they'd all have their bloody cameras. What a shame the back-up dogs couldn't get here as quickly. The other bad news he saw was a small minivan tucked in between two large open hangers.

He called it in, and Maxine said that would be the van full of mystery men that the police at the meeting had said was seen in Tennant Creek, the one that had disappeared.

'Well, that's not going to help us here, is it dearest?'

Maxine thought, *I wish he would be a bit more ... well, I don't know ... giving me a solid message about what it is he is conveying when he talks to me like that. Is he that bloody dumb? Maybe we will all die here today, and none of it will matter. But I'll go to my grave having loved him all of my life. The shame of it will be the idiot will never have known.*

CHAPTER FORTY-ONE

Riley was in his element. Not only was he flying, but he was in his favourite space, the open space of the Australian outback. From up above where he was, the view was simply magnificent as were the sounds of silence, that haunting silence of this unimaginable, vast, mysterious land, a land seen by some as unforgiving and extreme, and by others like Riley and Maxine as unspoiled beauty where nature rules. He wondered how you could even begin to explain the outback to a city slicker. Riley's image of the outback was something he only got when he daydreamed, and he could explain it no other way.

Yes, he said to himself, *I love this sunburnt country. However, by now, somebody, you would think, would have alerted the authorities that either a movie was being made at the old airfield, or there was some serious shit happening. Help could be on the way, but it needs to be better than just the Lone Ranger.*

'Go back and fire up that Land Cruiser,' he said over the radio. 'It will be battered with shrapnel but should still be okay to drive. We need to get to the mailboxes somehow without getting hit by that sniper. Park the Cruiser end-on-end with your vehicle along the front of the post office veranda. That should block the sniper's view. Draw straws to see who goes for the last two boxes. I'll do what I can from up here to protect you. Once you get the packages, hightail it for the police station. I'll be above, helping you along the way.'

Riley watched them drive back and pick up the Land Cruiser. Maxine had drawn the short straw and went to the mailboxes. Riley spotted the sniper on the roof. He dropped a grenade, which blew a hole in the roof, and the sniper was gone.

Maxine was at the second mailbox when a hail of bullets hit the two vehicles blocking the front of the veranda. Toby slid out the door with the rifle and threw a grenade over the top of the cars, giving Maxine a chance to get to cover behind the cars. The heavy fire was coming from the minibus which had come round from between the hangers. There were seven of them in the bus; the two firing automatic weapons from the sunroof of the bus had them pinned down. Both vehicles had more holes in them than Swiss cheese.

Riley was desperately trying to get close enough to drop a grenade on the bus but had to keep banking away to dodge the bullets. He knew they were down beside the car and would hear the radio from where they were.

'I can't get near them to drop a grenade. If you can hear me, fire a round in the air on three.'

One, two, bang!

'Okay. When I call out now, you count to five and open fire with three pumps of the shotgun. That should keep them inside the sunroof while I swing in with a door breaching pack.'

Toby fired another shot in the air. Riley flew in as close as he was game and called out, 'Now!'

He flew in over the bus in perfect timing to the count of five. Toby and Maxine opened up with a barrage of shotgun and rifle fire, and Riley dropped the door breaching pack as he passed over the bus, not quite as accurately as he would have liked, but it blew most of the left front bodywork off the bus and killed the bloke in the front passenger seat.

'Six left,' Riley said.

While the terrorists were regrouping, Toby and Maxine were in their now bullet-riddled vehicle with the five drone drug packages, heading down the old main runway. The goons had managed to start the bus and were spinning around to follow. The bus they were driving was a pusher, meaning the engine was in the rear and hadn't been affected. Most of the front of the bus had gone along with the windscreen, so the driver was visible and getting covered in the red dust the chopper rotors were sucking up from the road.

It wasn't long before the gunfire started again from the sunroof and Riley had to bank away over the Daly River Nature Park. He flew over the home of saltwater crocodiles, reptiles, wild pigs, water buffalo, the red kapok tree, the Nauiyu Aboriginal Community and the Merrepen Arts Centre, which enabled him to come up in front and to one side of the bus, almost unnoticed, before he started taking fire.

He was now flying sideways, backward from the front of the bus, a skill not all pilots possessed. He leant out of the perspex chopper bubble and shot the driver. He saw the passenger rip the dead driver from the seat and throw him out through the hole in the front of the bus. Quick as a flash, the bloke was behind the wheel. The sunroof twins were still firing blindly at the rear of Toby and Maxine's car, but apart from filling it with more air holes, not much damage was being done.

From above, Riley watched the chase. Toby was driving as they shot down the Daly River Road. Suddenly there it was – the police station. The vehicle did a perfectly executed three-hundred-and sixty-degree slide-in within a few feet of the front door. They punched in the code and disappeared. Riley watched them make it inside.

What to do now – stay and support the people that mattered here on the ground at the moment, or sneak off and leave them on the pretence of getting help? With the range of the Robinson chopper and the time it would take to get help and come back, his friends could all be dead. *Where was the bloody cavalry?*

Three high powered rounds split the plexiglass of the chopper cabin as he landed. He grabbed his hessian bag of goodies and shotgun, dived behind the old water tank across the road from the police station and checked what was left in the bag. *One stun grenade, a door breaching pack and twenty shotgun shells – that might be enough support to get me into the building,* he thought. The police station was half-hidden among the trees, and the spinifex grass hadn't been cut down so there was at least some cover as he crawled towards the back of the station, which was really just a house that had been converted and modified to suit.

Inside the police station, Toby and Maxine were preparing a welcome surprise for the goons. They had been into the armoury and found what they needed and used bits and pieces of whatever they could find to set up the traps. They secured the drone drug packages in the armoury and locked the door. Maxine used the roll of string she found in the office drawer to rig across the back door with a door demolition explosive pack. Toby had found a shed out the back with a small aluminium boat and some fishing gear and a powerful gas operated speargun. He fastened one end of the fishing line to the inside of the front door and the other end to the trigger of the now mounted speargun jammed in the passage door facing the front. Their weapons had been reloaded from the ammo in the armoury, and they were as ready as they would ever be.

While they were lying in wait, Maxine suddenly said, 'What if Riley tries to get in? He'll be blown to bits! I know him; he will try get in here somehow.'

'Yes, you're probably right. There's a window near each of the doors. I'll take the front; you've got the back. Anyone other than Riley comes, get back out of the way and let them come in,' Toby said.

Riley had been keeping count. He knew there were four goons left. One of them was trying to pin him down, and he had seen another getting over the side fence of the police station, but he had lost track of the other two. He skirted around in a wide circle, keeping low, past two jail cells and two outdoor showers just outside the cells. The showers had a chain that hung down inside the cells that turned the water on when it was pulled. The shower head could turn to face in or outside the cell. He saw an extension cord plugged into an outdoor socket on the main building. He pulled the plug off the end to expose the bare wires and ran the cord down to the bottom of the showers. He wrapped the bare wires around the base of the showers, pulled the chain and the showers came on. He went back and turned on the power, hid behind the cells and waited.

'He's not over here,' the one over the side fence called out.

The goon following Riley called back, 'Meet me at the cells and we'll both bust in through the back door. I'll turn the shower water off on the way past.'

He reached over, stood in the water and pulled. He shook and vibrated as two hundred and forty volts of electricity shot through his body. His eyeballs shot out and hung down his face on thin optic nerves. Smoke was coming from underneath his fingernails and Riley could smell his skin burning.

Riley decided to let the other goon try the back door first. If it looked like he was going to get in, Riley would shoot him. But when the goon opened the back door. Maxine having laid the explosive door breaching charges down low, they blew the goon's feet clean off the ends of his legs. He crawled back out with his feet hanging on bits of skin and bone trailing behind him. Riley shot him in the head.

Maxine called out, 'Is that you, Riley? Hurry up and get in here.'

He slid in through the door and they locked it.

There's still two of them left out there,' he said.

CHAPTER FORTY-TWO

Penny and Bazza were waiting to hear about the diamond drug payment arrangements, but if the cavalry came barging in, the information would be lost.

'Quick,' she said to Bazza, 'Go back and stop them from coming in. I'll stay and listen in. Information about these diamond payments must have been the transmission we heard when we came in, in that foreign language.'

'I'm going, he said, 'but you be careful. As soon as you get the information, get out of here and we'll drop the grenades.'

'So, tell me the arrangements,' the goon said to the radio operator.

'The message came from someone called The Syndicate, and is as follows: your contact is Mick, Alpha, Tango, Stop. Hotel, India, Lima, Delta, Alpha. Stop. At Wallaroo, Stop.'

'Okay,' he said. 'Let's get out of here. Get the others and we'll use the emergency exit tunnel.'

Penny heard the entire conversation and headed for the mine's entrance where the SWAT team were waiting with Bazza for her.

The SWAT team commander called out, 'Drop the explosives down the air vents.'

There were a few seconds of silence, then the underground erupted and anyone or anything that was still down there was obliterated. They went into a huddle to exchange what they knew so far. Penny gave them the coded message which they all agreed made no sense.

But Penny said, 'Why do I know that name, Wallaroo? I've heard that name since I've arrived here in the outback. And who or what is The Syndicate? Someone, get me all we have on them. We will all meet again in the major incident room briefing room at the Tennant Creek police station at nine o'clock tomorrow.'

The next morning as Penny entered the foyer of the police station, there was a man in a wheelchair admiring a small black windmill standing among the indoor ferns.

'Hello. Can I help you?'

'My name is Zach and I'm admiring the windmill that I made. I see someone has plumbed it into a small water tank and now it pumps water to the ferns.'

'You're very clever,' Penny said, 'and you gave it to the police station.?

'Well, that's not quite how it happened. Let's just say there was a golden opportunity that's now been missed.'

She didn't know what that meant, but she said, 'Have a nice day' and went into the meeting.

She told one of the policeman she had just been talking to someone in a wheelchair called Zach.

He said, 'Is he here, is he? That reminds me, we need to go get his Land Rover from Double Diamond. I'll tell you the story later.'

'Thank you for your attendance again,' Penny said to everyone. 'Get yourselves a coffee and we will hear from this detective who has done the research on whoever this Syndicate is.'

'Thank you,' he said. 'What I'm about to tell you is the latest intelligence that the Australian Secret Intelligence Service has on The Syndicate. They are a worldwide crime organisation, an army of darkness that deals in drugs, money laundering, contract killing, human trafficking and generally anything that is unlawful. They have no headquarters, or if they do, it is a well guarded secret. They deal mainly on the dark web and on coded untraceable phones. Their numbers are unknown but among them are high-ranking civilian and military officials, such as police, doctors and lawyers, all the way down to the scum of the earth, thieves, murderers, cutthroats and psychos. They tend to be more active in Europe, America and places like France. ASIS has no idea what connection they would have with anything to do with Tennant Creek and the Double Diamond cattle station. They certainly wouldn't have gone into cattle rustling ...' (Everyone laughed, although none of this was a laughing matter). 'ASIS also says that they have started infiltrating into worldwide companies and placing dormant syndicate operatives within those companies ready when called upon. They will dig up some dirt on an employee or their family and use that as leverage for The Syndicate's benefit. Sometimes they have paid for families' expensive life-saving operations to blackmail them into unlawful actions. Is there anyone here smarter than me who can say with some certainty what the hell they would want here in Tennant Creek? And before I forget, ASIS are of the opinion that what has been happened here over the last few months is to do with three totally different organisations with different agendas.'

'Now I know where I've heard that name,' Penny said, 'the Wallaroo Pastoral Company. They're the lease managers for the Roper family at Double Diamond. They are based in New Zealand, so what they have to do with all this is a mystery to me.'

At the end of the meeting, one detective said, 'There's only one station that's been involved in all of this. The coded information we received means we now know where they are going but not who the contact is. We all need to put our heads together and sort out the rest of that phonetic alphabet code.'

Bazza said, 'Have we tried putting the letters together?'

They wrote them down on the whiteboard – MATHILDA.

'Means nothing,' someone said.

Penny said, 'I think the problem is we are trying to solve something that's not there. Try the KISS principle – "keep it simple, stupid". Let's have another go, and this time, follow the inductions by using the stops.'

MAT. HILDA.

'Someone's name.'

'That's right, Penny said. 'It's the Double Diamond manager's name from the Wallaroo Pastoral Company in New Zealand.'

CHAPTER FORTY-THREE

Back at Double Diamond, Matilda was beginning to wonder if he had given in to the secret caller in New Zealand too easily. He had been a loyal and trusted employee with the Wallaroo Pastoral Company for twenty-five years, but on his job application, he hadn't been quite honest when it came to the family history section on the form: his brother was in jail. The anonymous caller had said a letter would be going to the company if he didn't play ball. The caller had known he was on his way to Australia to a cattle station called Double Diamond. They wanted him to be the courier of a small sack of diamonds that eventually would be collected at the station. He was told it would be a simple assignment, and he would hear from them no more.

He was having second thoughts about it now, but he didn't know what he could do. The Roper family were good people, in particular Maxine and her sister, and although he wasn't family, he had been treated as such. In the beginning, it seemed like such a small request to be a courier to Australia in return for their silence, but events had got out of hand – there had been many deaths since his arrival – and he didn't want to further endanger them.

The diamonds were safely hidden in the bed in his cabin. His bed had four hollow brass posts that the mosquito net hung from. The top of the posts had a brass knob that he had removed, stuffed in the diamonds and replaced the knob. He needed to talk to someone, but they were all away investigating the bombing of the aircraft, the deaths and burning of the buildings at the station. He was now convinced that he and the diamonds were in some way responsible and caught up in the mess. He had thought about clearing out but decided to stay and face the music, however loud that might be.

* * *

The Daly River police station was surrounded by trees and long grass that made it easy to reach the front door without being seen. The goon was smiling as he carefully and quietly opened the door. The last sound he heard was the swoosh of the gas canister as it shot the spear through his neck. His tongue shot out and was bitten off when his teeth came crunching down with the shock. His eyeballs were sucked deep into his skull, leaving two empty sockets.

'So now there's only two left out there somewhere,' Riley said.

'They might give up and go,' said Maxine.

'Fat chance,' said Toby. 'These people would kill their own mother. They're not going anywhere while they know we're in here.'

'Is all this killing worth it?'

'The price of doing what's right is never too high,' Toby said.

They left the two goons' bodies at the front and back doors as a warning to what happened if they tried to get in. It would be dark soon, and that would make it easier for the goons to move around without being seen. They rigged the back door again with one of the shotguns. The back of the building would be the darkest while the front was fairly well lit by the four flood lights mounted under the veranda.

Riley decided they needed the high ground advantage. He climbed onto the roof in the dark at the back of the building with two grenades and his 9mm pistol. He would be able to see anyone trying to come in at the back.

Toby said, 'I don't think they will come through the doors now when they see what happened to the others, but we need to spike the windows.'

Checking the windows were locked, they found as many glass bottles and drinking glasses as they could, broke them into pieces and laid them along the inside of the window ledges. Toby would monitor the left windows and Maxine the right. They turned off all the inside lights and left the front flood lights on.

It was now a waiting game.

Bazza said, 'Now, before I say anything, I know I am only Water Police, and if you pardon the pun, out of my depth, but I think if anyone is going back out to Double Diamond, they shouldn't be bursting in guns blazing. This Matilda person might not even be involved, and even if he is, we don't want to scare off or spoil the goons' plans to go out there for the diamonds.'

'Spoken like a true policeman,' said one detective, 'obviously not all Water Police are wet behind the ears.'

'Touché,' said Bazza. 'So, how will we do this? We need some sort of cover story. I've never been out there, so nobody knows me.'

'You would barely be in their way by yourself if they came in numbers,' Penny said.

'Barely is better than nothing,' he said, 'and back-up is only an hour's flying time for help.'

'It might just work. We will borrow overalls from the local tow truck mob and give you the necessary paperwork that will give you the authority to pick up Zach's car. Someone can drive you out there. You will make sure the car won't start and stay there until someone comes for the diamonds. There will only be one person who will know who you are, which means we need to find out where Maxine is. The last I heard was that she went with Senior Sergeant Riley, following the trail of the five packages from Double Diamond to Daly Waters. There's a police station at Daly River. It's not manned twenty-four hours, but I'll try the number; you never know.'

* * *

'The phone that's ringing, it'll be our side, not theirs,' Toby said.

He picked up the phone.

'This is Detective Inspector Penny Jane. We are looking for Maxine Roper who is travelling with Senior Sergeant Riley in your area. Have you seen them, and who am I speaking to?'

'Well, well, the prodigal family have made contact. This is Inspector Tobias and yes, they are both here. We have been under attack all day and our plea for help went unanswered. Please tell me you're just outside the police station!'

'We would now obviously love to be but we are not, and we were not aware of your need for back-up. Hang in there. Help is definitely now on the way. I know this is a bad time, but I need to speak to Maxine. We are having our own bad time at this end, and she can assist in the action of our plans at Double Diamond.'

She gave Maxine the outline of the plans and said there would be no problem with Riley and Toby knowing. The important part was the secrecy at Double Diamond while the undercover cop was there.

Penny notified the relevant authorities and within the hour, three patrol cars and a police helicopter arrived, and the last two goons were shot dead. They all stayed the next two days at the pub while the final briefing and reports were done. A bandage repair job was done on the chopper's plexiglass cabin, the engine and moving parts were checked over and the little Robbie was refuelled.

*   *   *

The young girl in the radio shack called out to Matilda, 'There's a radio message come through for you: "Brother coming from New Zealand for birthday to see camel races at Boulia outback Queensland weekend 18–20 July. Looking forward to seeing you. Bring him his present, and wear your red silk scarf." It would be nice to see your brother but today is the eleventh, so you'll need to leave straight away if you're going.'

Matilda said to himself, *Yes, that would be nice if I had a brother*, but he knew that it was all about the diamond delivery. He had no choice now. He would have to go.

'Car coming,' she said.

He could see the red dust cloud in the distance. As it got closer, they could see it was a police Land Cruiser.

Maybe they already know I've got the diamond. No, how could they know that? Stop panicking, he told himself.

The driver was a policeman, and the passenger was someone from a towing company in Tennant Creek who said he was there to pick up a vehicle belonging to Zach.

'No problems,' said Matilda. 'The old Land Rover is in the vehicle barn with the other workers' vehicles.'

The police driver said he wouldn't be staying and was driving back now.

Matilda said, 'That's a bit of luck. I'm going on leave. If I get a ride back with you, I'll get a hire car at Tennant Creek.'

'Of course you can,' he said, 'but be quick about it. I'm leaving in thirty minutes.'

Matilda shot back to his cabin, packed a small bag and unscrewed the bed post brass top to get the small bag of diamonds. As he was pulling them out of the tight brass tubing, two diamonds fell out of the sack to the bottom of the bed post. He didn't have time to tip the bed end upside down to get the diamonds back, so he decided they would be staying. No one would ever know that he had given this station the real meaning of its name, Double Diamond.

As he got in the car, he said, 'Do you mind going about twenty kilometres out of your way so I can drop off some supplies for the station at the drovers hut?'

'No problems,' the driver said.

Bazza saw the person he had come to watch disappear in a cloud of red dust.

'I need to send an urgent radio message,' he told the young radio operator. 'Can we link to the police frequency?'

'No, but we can go via the Flying Doctor network.'

*   *   *

At Daly Waters, Riley and Maxine said their goodbyes and lifted off. They would puddle jump and refuel along the way via Elliott back to Tennant Creek. Toby's narcotics vehicle was full of holes and on the back of a truck, so he was going back to Tennant Creek in one of the highway patrol cars, a four-hundred-kilometre road trip.

Once they were all back at Tennant Creek, Penny had brought them up to date with plans that were now no value with Matilda gone to Boulia.

'That's where we need to be, she said, 'once we get Bazza back from the Double Diamond. We have been given approval by the air wing for Riley to fly us there in one of the Cessna 550 Citations, capable of carrying six passengers and two pilots if required. They have a range of nearly three thousand kilometres and, given that Tennant Creek to Boulia by road is roughly a thousand kilometres, we can be there and back without refuelling, but that decision will be Riley's. We need to be on site the afternoon of Friday the eighteenth. Today is the fifteenth, so no time to lose.'

Riley said, 'Right, who's going?'

'Clark, Robo, Bazza, Maxine, myself and the only one Matilda doesn't know, Toby. He will be the one on our side wearing the red silk scarf to convince Matilda to hand over the diamonds. That's what the instructions were in the message the radio operator gave us. That leaves room for your copilot.'

'We don't need a copilot, Riley said. 'The flying time doesn't require it, and I want Maxine in that seat. I'll go back now in the Robbie and get Bazza. Get yourselves organised. To bring Bazza back, sorry, but there's no room for you, Maxine, my dear.'

She still didn't know what he meant, but she liked it.

CHAPTER FORTY-FIVE

The police finalised their plans at a last meeting on the day before they left and, as was expected of her, the profiler had done the background homework as to location, forward planning and probable outcomes.

She said, 'The Syndicate, if that's who this is, have chosen this location and timing to coincide with the outback camel races at Boulia. It is a small outback town in the land of the min min light, which is an unexplained aerial phenomenon of a glowing light or orb that is reported to follow people at a distance in the outback. This little town and its racecourse will overnight turn into a thriving metropolis with thousands of tourists in tents, trailers, caravans and motorhomes. The two day-and-night event starts on the Friday night with live shows, music, dancing and market stalls. There are camel races all day Saturday, with the winners racing in the big race on Sunday called the Cup, a fifteen-hundred-metres long race. The jockeys sit behind the hump on small pads with no reins, and the camels steer themselves down the track.'

'Well, we might as well all make the most of it while we're there and have a bet with the bookies,' said Toby.

'You, my friend,' said Penny, 'will be busy wearing the red silk scarf to scam the diamonds off Matilda, if our doozy double works. The hard part will be finding the goons among the crowd. I wouldn't think they will be wearing a red scarf to tell us who they are. They'll convince Matilda to hand over the diamonds with a gun in his face.'

They loaded their personal gear, sleeping swags, camping gear and small heximine stoves. Their police ration packs were as the same as army ration: a small round tin of cheese, a small block of chocolate, a teabag, a single serve coffee packet, a packet each of instant beef stew and chicken pasta, instant mash potatoes, a fruit bar, crackers, plastic utensils and matches.

Riley said. 'Maxine, I'm sitting you up front with me, my love.'

This time he did see her blush.

'I know you want to learn how to fly, to be the only outback flying veterinarian, and when all this is over, I will teach you how to fly the Double Diamond's small two-seater Cessna. But for now, you're my copilot. Make the announcement.'

She switched on the mike, put the headphones on and said, 'Good afternoon, lady and gentlemen. Welcome aboard Flight Silk Scarf to Boulia. Please note the captain has the seatbelt light on. The flying time is two hours and your captain is the invincible Riley. We will be taking the scenic route today, taking off eastbound for Mount Isa, then swinging south over the top of Julia Creek, Cloncurry, Winton and Longreach, swinging west into the lovely outback sunset to begin our decent into Boulia. Sit back and relax. The wine of your choice will be served on arrival along with the crackers in your ration pack.'

Everyone laughed and clapped.

She read out the cockpit check list. 'Ailerons, rudders and elevators, all check okay with free movement. Trim controls adjusted and functioning correctly. All control locks removed and stowed away. We are good to go, Captain. I'll continue the inflight checks when we are airborne as required.'

'Okay,' he said, 'and now we are airborne. Wheels up, thank you.'

She flicked the switch and said, 'Wheels are up, sir.'

On arrival, they did a circuit over the town and racecourse.

'Look at the amount of people, tents, vans, and vehicles down there,' Toby said.

The racecourse was not in a separate area but was integrated within the town. The airport's small passenger terminal building, with long open verandas open at each end, sat in a vast open space of red dirt. The end of the runway ran off into the outback off to infinity.

'The population here is about two hundred,' said Penny, 'but from the air now looks like two thousand.'

Riley could have taxied the aircraft almost anywhere he wanted in the open areas, but he parked the plane with the big blue letters that read "Police" away from the terminal building where they wouldn't have to mix with other campers and could set up camp and get a fire ready for the night with the wood they had brought with them for just that occasion. However, it wasn't unusual at events like this to see a police presence. The difference here was that the local police were all in uniform whereas they were in civilian clothes like everyone else.

Saturday was uneventful. They split up and wandered about, watching the different camel racing events.They had all been issued with ear pod communication and had kept in touch with each other throughout the day. Some of the events were long walking distances apart, so by the end of the day, they were all buggered. They had seen nothing out of the ordinary and nobody had seen any sign of Matilda.

Toby had taken a photo on his phone of one of the bookies' boards to show the others.

'Look at these camel names and the odds. Curly the camel ten to one, Clumsy Camel six to one, Lumpy four to one, Humpback two to one, Camelot eight to one, Caramel also four to one, Sandy Sultan three to one, Cuddly Camel nine to one, and Dune Buggy five to one. Someone's got a sense of humour.'

On Saturday night, there was live music with a band and a male and female singer. The younger crowd were dancing, or what Bazza said was more like wriggling, jiggling and groping. Penny accused him of having an old person's view of a young person's fun. Toby and his silk red scarf had been propositioned at least once with the comment, 'Hi there, Duckie. Love the scarf. I'll be at the dance tonight.' He would normally have knocked the bloke out, but under the circumstances he was limited to glaring at him.

They sat round the fire that night with the smell of the food stalls wafting through the air.

Riley said, 'This ration pack of mine isn't going to cut it. Who wants a hamburger?'

Six hands went up and six voices said, 'Yes, please.'

They drew a rough map in the red dirt and selected a spot for each of them that would cover the most ground. The area was so large it would still require them to have to move around, but within their own allocated radius of responsibility.

'Tomorrow is our last chance at this,' Penny said. 'I'm concerned we haven't seen Matilda yet. Maybe the delivery took place here before we arrived, or maybe I have read it all wrong and it has gone down somewhere else, and we've wasted our time.'

Bazza said, 'I'm sure you'll hear tomorrow that this is the meeting place. Don't worry, it just hasn't gone down yet. It's not over till the fat lady sings.'

CHAPTER FORTY-SIX

Sunday was the biggest day of the weekend, the main event being the Camel Cup. Toby said, for some reason, it felt and looked like a lot more people were there. He was the only one who didn't have a designated area, and he needed to cover as much ground as he could to find Matilda. If any of the others spotted Matilda, they would let Toby know. They needed to be careful not to be seen, as Matilda had seen them all at the station except Toby.

Maxine was sitting near the bookies area on a small metal drum she had found. She was wearing a large straw hat pulled down to cover her face. Matilda was walking towards her with his red scarf when she saw two men following behind and two more coming towards him. If they got to him first, it was all over. She rushed ahead and, making it look like she hadn't seen him, bumped into him and knocked him over. The four men sidestepped her and Matilda and watched from among the crowd at the bookies stand.

'Where are you, Toby? I need you at the bookies stand right now.'

'I'm behind the electronic betting board near you.'

'Well, get your arse over here and grab Matilda. He is the one on the ground with the red scarf. There are four of them and they are on to him. You need to be there now.'

Toby appeared as the four men grabbed Matilda and pulled him up. Toby elbowed his way in.

'Thank you for helping my friend up,' he said. 'That was decent of you.'

He grabbed Matilda, and they walked off with the goons trailing some distance behind. Maxine gave everyone an outline of what had just happened over their ear pods, and they all agreed to stay hidden within the crowd and to meet at the finishing line. The race was about to start, and that's where everyone would be.

A tourist there to see the race might have been disappointed. There were no raised seats or grandstands, just flat areas on the railed fence to stand, and nothing could be seen of the race until the camels went past. Not all of them did that, as some had a mind of their own, which is why the finishing post was the popular place for people to be, and the safest place for Toby and Matilda at this very moment. The rest of them needed to stay undetected by Matilda and the goons as long as was necessary for the success of the mission.

The goons watched as the man in the red scarf spoke to their own red scarf courier, and they saw the diamonds changing hands. A shot came from somewhere in the crowd and Matilda fell with a bullet to the head. Toby grabbed the small sack of diamonds, ducked down among the crowds' feet and crawled away. One of the goons standing on a picnic seat saw him crawling away. The bonus for Toby was he could communicate to his team where he was and what was happening through his ear pod.

'He has disappeared in the crowd. I've lost him,' Maxine said, 'and he has the diamonds. I don't know how many goons are here, but there are at least four that are following Toby.'

Toby worked his way along the rear of the pub marquee and snuck in through a flap at the back, bought himself a beer and stood among the men at bar.

'I'm in the pub marquee at the moment,' he said.

Bazza had seen two goons going into the pub marquee, so he followed them in. One goon waited at the canvas entrance; the other, who had recognised Toby, headed towards the bar.

Bazza said, 'Goon coming up now behind you.'

Toby turned.

In English that could barely be understood, the goon said, 'We want diamonds. You give now, or we kill.'

Toby felt about as useful as a one-legged man with a wheelbarrow. He couldn't shoot the bastard among the crowd or start a fight, so he smiled and said, 'Do your best, mate.'

The goon said, 'We wait outside.'

Outside the pub marquee was a crowd gathering to look at a dead man with his carotid artery cut while Bazza quietly walked off, folding up his favourite Tom Mix pocket knife.

Maxine had been watching the one standing on the picnic seat for some time. He had just been joined by two others dressed as security guards. She passed the information over the ear pod net that they were communicating on.

Riley came on and said, 'Two at the pub, three with Maxine, sounds like five of them.'

'Make that four now,' said Bazza. 'I'm following Toby to protect his rear. We will switch the diamonds, then split and get to the plane, if we can.'

Toby and Bazza bumped into each other, switched the diamonds and went their separate ways. Maxine had taken photos on her phone of three of the goons and given them to

Riley who was now sharing them with the local uniformed police after showing his badge.

The walk to the plane was over an unprotected two hundred metres of open space. Bunching up wouldn't be a good move, so they spread out twenty metres apart. Halfway to the plane, they could see behind them a vehicle trailing a cloud of red dust – not a good sign. A Toyota ute came into view with two goons standing in the back with weapons raised.

'Jesus, nowhere to go, nowhere to hide!' Riley said, 'Everyone, down, and shoot flat out at the windscreen on the driver's side.'

They waited till it was nearly too late, then started firing. A red stain appeared on the windscreen and the Toyota ute flipped into the air.

In the distance, coming fast, were several sets of red and blue flashing lights. They had to listen to the whinging of the police sergeant about being kept in the dark, which he took as a sign of no confidence in his local force and a bloody rude non-adherence to protocol.

'And look at the mess you're leaving behind!' he said.

'Well, Toby said, 'if you pray for rain, sometimes you have to deal with the mud, and sometimes to achieve peace, you need to prepare for war.'

CHAPTER FORTY-SEVEN

Maxine said, 'I don't know about anyone else, but after all this shit storm, I want to see these bloody diamonds.'

'Be my guest,' Bazza said and gave her the small cloth sack.

'No way!' she called out.

'What's wrong?'

'They're just plastic beads,' she said, and tipped them out into everyone's hand. 'Hang on. There's something written down.'

She read the tiny text: "For travellers needing help and support, the drovers hut is the diamond in the outback."

'What's all that mean?' Toby said. 'All this for plastic beads?'

'No, I don't think so,' said Penny. 'I think Matilda got cold feet and was trying to do the right thing and not bring the diamonds. He's lost his life but told us where the real diamonds are.'

'Well,' said Riley, 'that's why you're the profiler and I'm the pilot.'

'I suppose Maxine knows the location of this place?' said Bazza.

'Yes, she does,' said Riley.

'I sure do,' Maxine said, 'so why are we standing here burning daylight?'

Maxine played her role of the copilot on the return flight. By the time they were wheels down in Tennant Creek, it was late afternoon, just on dusk. A police divisional van loaded them in and took them to the Bluestone Motor Inn in Paterson Street. They had the evening meal together, got a drink at the bar and sat by the pool to discuss the next move.

*　*　*

Somewhere in Europe, a phone conversation was underway.

'We don't care how many people are dead,' the voice said, 'or are going to be dead. The Syndicate will not lose their diamonds for drugs they didn't get. They want them back. You have twenty-four hours.'

The four goons who had been on a twenty-four-hour stake-out of the police station since the aircraft had landed were watching the motel and had been given instructions to follow any movement that came from the police station.

*　*　*

At the meeting the next morning, it was decided the best way to the drovers hut was by vehicle, one hundred and twenty kilometres into the outback.

Riley said, 'You won't need Maxine and me for that. We have some serious time to start spending together, and the helicopter has to be returned to Double Diamond. I'm sure you'll manage without us.'

Bazza was released back to his unit of the Water Police in Darwin, and Toby returned to narcotics. Penny went back to Melbourne.

Two detectives headed off with directions to the drover's hut for the diamonds. The goons watched the bush track the police had taken. The map showed there was only one track that wound its way through the outback, crossing dry creek beds and gullies, so they were able to hang back out of sight. At one stage, they got too close to the car in front, so they pulled off the track next to a damp creek bed, got out and waited.

'Can you hear that?' one of the goons said. 'Something is coming. Holy Mary Mother of Jesus, what is that thing?'

'It must be the mythical Bunyip Man!' the other goon said. 'It looks like a ball of hair and fur with a set of wheels under it.'

'Well, whatever it is, I don't like it, and it's coming straight for us.'

They ran down the slope of the creek bed in an effort to reach the other side, but they immediately sunk to their knees. The more they moved and wriggled, the further they were sucked under into the red slime. They had obviously never heard the saying, "if you're in a hole, stop digging". In a month, the creek bed would be rock hard, but just after the wet season, it was six feet of red slime quicksand.

The Bunyip Man filled his motorbike with fuel from the car with the siphon hose he always carried as he watched them sink.

CHAPTER FORTY-EIGHT

At Double Diamond, Riley and Maxine towed the Cessna 150 two-seater aircraft out of the barn, washed it and filled it with aviation gasoline. The next morning, as promised, Riley began flying lessons with Maxine. They taxied out to the airstrip.

Riley said, 'Okay, Maxine, you're the left seat pilot; the copilot sits in the right seat. Pre-flight checks start now. Run your eye over the gauges; are they all working? Check fuel levels and confirm the mixture is rich. Set flaps at ten degrees for a short field take off like this one. Taxi to the centre runway, run the engines up to a moderate power setting and check the magneto and carburettor heat. Are you ready?'

'Yes.'

'Here we go. Smoothly advance the throttle to full power while holding the brakes. Release the brakes. Maintain a slightly low tail by pulling back slightly on the yoke. Watch the speed, fifty to sixty knots. Pull back now on the yoke, and up we go. Wheels up now. Maintain the best angle of climb and airspeed. Once you're happy with the altitude, retract the flaps and play among the clouds.'

She reached over and touched his hand. He smiled, squeezed her hand and gave her a cheeky wink. Maxine was beside herself. It was everything she had waited for for so long.

They over flew Tennant Creek and circled Lake Mary Ann, watching the population enjoying the lake, picnicking and swimming.

She said, 'We should be down there skinny dipping.'

Riley said, 'What a brazen hussy, Maxine!'

'I know.'

'How would you like to be my brazen hussy?'

'Oh, Riley, you fool, I love you bigger than big and have waited so long ... you will be my someone forever and a day, and if I ever lost you, I'd never find another you. I'm so sorry he said, I can't give you back the years you've lost, but I can make sure you don't loose anymore.'

Suddenly the engine spluttered and misfired.

Maxine said, 'We thought we'd removed all the sand from the tank.'

'What sand?'

'Some time ago, sand was put into all the vehicles and aircraft at the station by ... well, the rumour is by the Bunyip Man. We cleaned them all and changed the filters. There must still be some sand in the fuel line.'

'Well, whatever it is or who it was, we are going down.'

The Cessna hit the water in the middle of the lake with a thud and bobbed around for a while. They tried to get out but the aircraft's thin body had twisted badly on impact and the cockpit doors were hopelessly jammed. The Cessna began to sink.

The tears ran down her face. For the final time, Maxine said, 'I love you, Riley.'

As their eyes and lips met, they sank to the bottom of the lake.

Several witnesses who saw the plane come down said, as the plane was sinking, they thought they heard the sound of a motorbike in the trees by the lake, and you could be forgiven for thinking the sunset was simply saying its goodbye. When they raised the plane to the surface, there was no one there. There is no shortage of stories and myths from the Australian outback, the ghosts of Lake Mary Anne is no exception.

Or maybe it was just the wind.

EPILOGUE

There are many stories that come from the Australian outback. Some are fiction and some are true. Stories that are told by Aboriginal Elders to children around their campfires. Stories like this one, the Double Diamond and the Golden Windmill story. The hundreds of years old Aboriginal bunyip stories that scares the pants off the children. Stories that come from the Dreamtime. Myths and stories that were inspired by this wide brown land under starlit satin skies. Unique stories that are hard not to believe. Stories you knew weren't true but wished they were.

What do you think, a motorbike or just the wind in the trees?

www.ingramcontent.com/pod-product-compliance
Lightning Source LLC
Chambersburg PA
CBHW031238210726

48287CB00003B/817